THE FERAL BOY WHO LIVES IN GRIFFITH PARK

NEW MYTHS AND LEGENDS FROM THE WILDERNESS OF LOS ANGELES

by

TIM KIRK

with selected stories from

David Carpenter, Patrick Cooper, Tim Davis, Josh Lawson, Steve Newman, and Rob Zabrecky

The Feral Boy who lives in Griffith Park by Tim Kirk

ISBN: 978-1-949790-11-5

eISBN: 978-1-949790-12-2

Copyright © 2019 Tim Kirk

Excerpt from THE RUBBER ROOM written by Porter Wagoner. Published by Owepar Publishing, Inc and used by kind permission. All rights reserved.

"The Ballad of Casey Jones" (written by Wallace Saunders 1900, published by T. Lawrence Seibert and Eddie Newton, 1909)

"Sally Goodin" (traditional)

Layout and book design by Mark Givens

Cover artwork by Cynthia Kirk

First Pelekinesis Printing 2019

For information:

Pelekinesis, 112 Harvard Ave #65, Claremont, CA 91711 USA

www.pelekinesis.com

THE FERAL BOY WHO LIVES IN GRIFFITH PARK

New myths and legends from the wilderness of Los Angeles

by

TIM KIRK

with

David Carpenter
Patrick Cooper
Tim Davis
Josh Lawson
Steve Newman
and Rob Zabrecky

PRAISE FOR THE FERAL BOY WHO LIVES IN GRIFFITH PARK

"I've always thought of Griffith Park as L.A.'s Transylvania. Sure during the day - especially on a Sunday when everyone is barbequing (sic), listening to the congas or making love behind the old zoo - it's a carnival. But for many years I ran its hills late at night, under full moons and in fogs, sometimes accompanied by an owl and coyote, and believe me, another world lives there. The Wild Boy is real and you will relish these Borges-like gems of story-telling."

–Mike Davis, author of *City of Quartz*

"I loved reading this weird and wonderful anthology. The stories are so beautifully written; I felt a visceral reaction to so much of the imagery. If you grew up in Greater Los Angeles, you will get this so hard. If you didn't, this book will make you feel like you did."

–Jane Wiedlin, The Go-Go's

For Dave, Patrick, Tim, Josh, Steve, and Rob.
Let's start a band!

CONTENTS

PREFACE

GRIFFITH PARK ISN'T A PHYSICAL SPACE.

Sure, I can drive to it, walk to it – it's that close. Within its 4000-plus acres are live oak trees that are centuries old. Driving through the park on solid asphalt roads, you'll pass the zoo I visited with my parents, the Old Zoo site where I partied, all three (!) little train rides that I rode endlessly with my toddler.

Yet the geography exists mainly in my mind. I found a rock with a plaque dedicating an overgrown thatch of bush as "Pepperland." It honors some anniversary of the release of the Beatles' Sgt. Pepper's album. I found a marker planted flat on the ground about a dozen yards from nothing. It remembers the dead in a protest of the Berlin Wall.

Or did I dream this?

Griffith Park is fertile ground for myth-making. Just like the city that surrounds it, and the state where it lives.

Let's remember that California existed long before it was discovered in the physical realm. It existed in a story. A romance novel written in Spain in 1510 by Garci Rodriguez de Montalvo featured the Island of California where the women were strong and black and rode Griffins with golden bridles. It was such a big hit that when explorers' ships bumped into the beaches of the Western shores their first thoughts were "Oh, here it is. Here's California."

Is it a surprise then that one of the most enduring myths is that, one day, a great earthquake will separate California from the coast and it will, indeed, be an island?

Now it's my turn to plant a seed.

There is a boy who lives in Griffith Park.

THE BOY

I T WAS NIGHT WHEN FIRE FELL FROM THE SKY AND RIPPED A GASH IN THE WOODS. No one was there to see it except for the boy. In the morning, he climbed up from the valley below and smelled the smoke and the dank upturned earth. He touched the burnt trees and rubbed the black ash between his palms. There was a crater, so deep that he couldn't see the bottom. Heat rose and felt warm against his naked body.

He stood for a long time, staring at the gaping hole, at the rising sun, and the hole again. And then he returned to his home alone in the rocks.

Trees grew and covered the scar long before the first people came. Thick weeds obscured the hole as a city grew around it. The hill became a park, the park became crisscrossed with hiking paths and horse trails, a carousel spun and vendors sold ice cream from refrigerated carts. People came and went and, at some point, they began to talk about the feral child that lived in Griffith Park.

SHARDS

1973

SYBIL ALWAYS WRITES IN HER JOURNAL AFTER HER POWER-WALKS AND SHE OFTEN WRITES ABOUT SKYE. She finds that the endorphin-fueled energy provokes an almost compulsive honesty which is both exhilarating and dangerous. She pours her thoughts into her journal, always afraid where they will take her, afraid mostly of reaching a degree of self-knowledge that will destroy her.

Today, she goes further and faster than ever before. Through the Old Zoo, rushing past the abandoned, rusting cages, up the steep trail lined with scrub oak to the top of Bee Rock, then around the landfill and down. She is nearly running as she hits the carousel. Sweat soaks her short-cropped hair and her baggy UCLA t-shirt hangs loose. She finds her favorite spot under her favorite tree and opens her journal on her favorite rock and begins to write.

She knows right away that she's going to end up writing about *him*. She decides to put it off as long as possible, by writing about everything else. It's a lot. She writes about her job search, about her car troubles, about the dentist appointment she keeps putting off. She writes about how good it was to see her brother during his lay-over at LAX. She starts to write about a conversation she had with Jacqueline, but Jacqueline is Skye's mother, so she quickly scurries away from that thought.

She writes about her accident instead. This is painful. She tends to avoid thinking about it. It's been three years. She'd been rushing from Venice, speeding on the 10, hurrying to join a group of friends for dinner in Hollywood. She'd only had the VW bus for a few weeks and wasn't used to not looking over a hood, and how close she was to the cars in front of her. This led to sudden braking, which led to a violent rear-ending, which led to smashing into the convertible. She would have followed her little dog, Gigi, through the windshield if the steering wheel column hadn't snapped and run her through.

She remained conscious during the calm after the crash, before people came running from their cars, before the sirens started wailing, before the paramedics arrived. She hung, impaled, listening to the radio. An Elton John song was playing, "Your Song."

It remained in heavy rotation the whole summer, reminding her always of that suspended moment.

She writes about the break-up with Wendy. She finds herself drifting back to the last really good week they spent together, on the film shoot out in the desert near Bishop. The film was a western and Wendy played a proper young lady from back East, the new wife of the local sheriff. She didn't have many scenes in the film, but she had to be on call the whole time. Wendy and Sybil developed a routine. Wendy would report for costume and make-up in the morning. Then she would borrow a walkie-talkie and join Sybil for long walks in the Alabama Hills near the set. The days would grow warm and they'd sit in the shadows of the rock formations, holding hands and talking. In her frills and lace and full make-up, Wendy looked more beautiful than ever.

Sybil glances at the page and realizes she's written a full paragraph on the way Wendy's hair looked in the desert light. She counts the times she used the word "ravishing." Eleven.

Wind turns pages in her hands. She looks up and the boy is

there.

He's standing a dozen feet away, bent slightly at the waist, breathing heavily. He is naked and burnt dark by the sun. A fine film of red dust covers his olive skin and the black mass of hair that hangs over his shoulders.

Slowly he catches his breath and he straightens and becomes very still. He's small, maybe three feet tall. His eyes are big and they lock on hers.

Sybil stares too. A small tremor travels from the top of her head to her toes.

She wonders if they are alone. A couple stands in the parking lot, talking. She can't hear a word they're saying. She realizes the wind is howling.

The boy's lips part but otherwise he does not move. She feels her breathing slow. She feels her mouth open, mirroring his.

There's a loud crack. A ragged branch rips from a tree and flies over her head, tumbling across the grass and then disappearing over a hill.

The boy is gone.

The wind suddenly drops and she can hear the couple loud and clear. *"That was the plan!"* *"No you assumed that was the plan. We've talked about your assumptions."* It's an argument.

She turns back to her journal and, in a fever, writes the truth about Skye. He's a monster. He hurts other children. He makes her play scary games. She wants to run away from him.

The truth is that she is trapped. She's in a deep pit and it took her a long time to slide down into it. At first, she would sit for Jacqueline, watching the child for a few hours, just like anyone would do for a friend. When she lost her job, Jacqueline started paying her. It was awkward for Sybil at first, but they were friends and Jacqueline was a busy studio executive raising a baby alone, she needed the help. The accident sapped her savings, so when the eviction notice came, she accepted Jacqueline's offer to move into one of the guest rooms. It made sense. She could help with Skye more easily there. Jacqueline told her they had a bond, Sybil and Skye.

Sybil remembers the first time she held Skye. Jacqueline's big house in Laurel Canyon was filled with people and music. All their friends were gathered to take up the noble cause. Jacqueline danced to Fleetwood Mac in a bright cotton dress which seemed to float around her as she spun. Sybil remembers looking at the golden-haired baby, feeling great gratitude that this was a world where he could get a second chance. She had lifted him high, joining in a warm stream of love that flowed around them all. "Skye The Magnificent," his mom called him. Jacqueline had rescued this child from a world of poverty and neglect. He would be raised in a world of wealth and privilege. Jacqueline was a single woman. He would have only one parent, but an enormous family of friends who would love him. And Sybil was one of them.

They've all stopped coming. Now, she meets Jacqueline at the door in the evening with a freshly bathed Skye and a forced smile. She dutifully reports the wondrous achievements of the precocious toddler and the incredible future that his burblings portend. Then she retreats to her room, dreading the possibility of an impromptu late night gab-fest. *Just us girls. Talking about our boy.*

* * *

Since that afternoon, Sybil leaves things for the boy. She places them on the rock where she saw him for the first and only time.

A coloring book. Some pencils and an eraser. A Brady Bunch lunch box. A Donald Duck sweatshirt. Some flip-flops.

She circles her favorite shows in the TV Guide, things she thinks he would like, but she never leaves it. She can't imagine he'd have any way to watch them.

RIVERSIDE RANCHO

1947

Rainin' an' a-pourin' an' the creek's runnin' muddy,
An' I'm so dam' drunk I can't stand steady,
I'm goin up the mountain an' marry little Sally,
Raise corn on the hillside an' the devil in the valley.
                    — *"Sally Goodin" Traditional*

T HE WALLS ARE THIN IN THE QUONSET HUT THAT MADDIE AND
HER PARENTS CALL HOME. So thin that she can hear the sounds of
other GI kids playing outside, even over the rasp of her neighbor's fiddle.

"What ya think, Billy?"

"Real interesting. Let me sing with it a bit."

Some raucous scatting joins the fiddle. Maddie doesn't mind.
Her parents won't be home from work for several hours. It takes
two trolleys and a long walk through Griffith Park to get to the
site of Rodger Young Village.

Besides, even though she's fifteen, she doesn't like being outside when it's dark. The other kids tease her that she's afraid of
the woods that surround the village and they are right. They quit
their games when they see her hurry inside and they chant "Bug-
Bear, BugBear" or "Maddie is afraid the BugBear will get her."
And they are right.

"Let me take it for a bit, Walter."

Walter puts down his fiddle and the singer picks up on the tune on guitar. Walter's wife works with Maddie's mom and dad at the Northrop factory down in Hawthorne. Walter plays at some club on Riverside and maybe for the movies. At least that's what Maddie has surmised from overheard conversations between Walter and his wife or the occasional visitor, like this guy with the guitar and the voice that takes her back to Oklahoma.

I ride along with my eye on the cattle but my head in the sky, there's a city over them mountains, and I'll see it by-and-by. Just rope them sorry doggies, and keep the bulls in line, this lonesome trail will end someday, by-and-by.

"That's pretty good, Billy."

"I'll have the rest by tonight. Or I'll just make something up on the spot."

"The Billy Clover special! It's your gift, brother."

"Yeah, and my curse. Things come so easy when I'm up there. Makes me wonder why I bother with anything else. I should just wake up and step on stage. That's the only place I feel alive."

"What about the ladies, Billy?"

"Oh, they're up there with me. Pretty girls and sex and that feeling you have after a full course meal or your third beer. Everything all at once."

"Sounds like church."

"The holy church of Riverside Rancho!"

Lying in bed is the worst. The camp is quiet and she can hear that muffled creaking sound in the woods. Like someone walking on an old mattress with wooden shoes. The BugBear.

She wishes they'd just give up and go back home.

They've been waiting for over a year. Dad was stationed in the Pacific and one of the last GIs to be transferred back to the states. By the time he'd loaded up the house and his wife and Maddie and driven the long road to Los Angeles, the waiting list for housing on the GI Bill was a mile long. He'd have to wait while people with names like Taper and Kaiser build houses in places with names like Lakewood, City of Temple, Panorama City. They are going up fast—a block or more a week. But there are a lot of people waiting.

In the meantime, Maddie's family and the rest of the GI transplants live in Rodger Young Village, the community of 750 military surplus Quonset huts the army had set up on the old airfield in the upper East corner of Griffith Park.

"I sing 'by-n-by' to the restless herd, so deep in this valley all alone, will I ever find that golden city, or will the trail just lead back home."

She got to the club early. She'd crossed the park while it was still light out. It had been an uneventful walk, even a nice one. The trees were in bloom and there was a gentle breeze. But she dreads the walk home in the dark. And the angry parents waiting for her when she gets there. She'd left a note but that won't be enough. She's sure.

The club stands alone, no homes or buildings around it, just like a dance hall on a dusty country road. Maddie feels exposed— she's the only one there. But quickly, they begin to arrive. An hour before the show, and the sidewalk out front is full of people. Some are girls just a little older than her. Girls with jobs and boyfriends and pretty long skirts that look just like Home but aren't quite.

Her heart races as the crowd grows and moves around her,

laughing and flirting and showing off their fancy duds, over-flowing onto the two lanes of Riverside Blvd. Two blocks from the entrance to the park and it feels like downtown on New Years' Eve.

She keeps her eyes fixed on the large brick chimney that dominates the exterior of the club. The chimney reminds Maddie of her Gramma Etta's place back in Ratliff City, except this one is huge and has lighted letters reading "Rancho Dancing." The lights also spell out "Cocktails" which would be a hoot to see on Gramma's chimney.

The image of Etta standing on her porch in her well-worn apron holding a freshly baked pie in one hand and a martini glass in the other makes Maddie laugh, and, like that, the doors open and she is swept inside.

The first night at Riverside Rancho is a blur. She is mostly aware of the crowd two-stepping and doing something she learns later is called the Lindy Hop. She knows they must be serving drinks somewhere in the giant crowded room because almost everyone is holding one. There is the music. There is shouting over the music.

And there is Billy. Resplendent in his white cavalry bib shirt with fine red embroidery, Billy floats like a shining beacon above the surging mass of dancers and through the haze of cigarette smoke that hangs over their heads.

That light captures Maddie's gaze and won't let go.

Billy stands still, legs spread, lightly swinging as he plays. The stage is large but his Clover Boys are all packed tightly around him—the other two guitarists, stand-up bass player, drummer, saxophonist and Walter on fiddle—like they too are feeling his magnetic pull.

He sings about girls with names like "Sunbonnet Sue" and

"Nancy Jane," about places she knows like Tulsa and Wichita, and about places she doesn't know like Cowtown and T'Juana. There is plenty of fiddle and Billy always nods appreciatively at Walter as he plays. He sings about a cabin on a hill which started the audience cheering before he hits the chorus, and everyone loves it so much he plays it again.

"There's a cabin in the hills, no sight is ever prettier, than the view from her win-der, with lovely Susie by my side, and a pinto pony hitched out back, out back of a cabin in the hills."

The park is dark. The only light comes from a sliver of moon and the faint residual glow of the surrounding city. All the music has left a din in her ears and she is happy for the company. But the din fades and then it's just dark and so, so quiet.

The pavement disappears just past the little clearing they call Crystal Springs and with it the last of the scattered picnic tables. She hadn't realized how comforting their occasional appearance had been. She turns onto the dirt path that leads for a mile through the woods to the village. She feels completely alone.

Except not.

A rustle. Cracking branches. A whistle? Breathing?

She tries to imagine rabbits burrowing in the hedges, hawks and sparrows settling into nests for the night, little mice and agile squirrels, a gentle wind. It doesn't work. All she can imagine, everywhere and all around her, is the BugBear.

Sometimes he is small, about her size, with long, long arms that touch the ground when he stands. Sometimes he is huge and hunched, crushing everything in his path with tremendously strong legs. Sometimes hairy. Sometimes hairless and smooth. But always "He."

The fiddling session starts late the next day, after noon. By then the pain in her behind has nearly vanished. Her return home had been less of a scene than she had feared. There had been half-hearted talk about curfews and other punishments, but her parents had settled on a few uninspired swats. The truth is that they were tired, too tired to really imagine having to punish her, let alone control her.

"How do you act crazy?"

"Just keep on drinking," answers Walter. "Gimme that."

The sound of sloshing. Maddie imagines they are passing a bottle between them, their instruments set aside for now.

"I was doing some work this morning out at the Columbia Ranch. Backing up Smiley Burnette on a couple of numbers for a Durango Kid flick. We were playing a number about a looney bird and Smiley is doing a schtick where he's running around with a big net trying to catch the thing."

"I can picture it."

"Yeah, he's hilarious. At the end, Smiley is supposed to put the net over one of us in the band and that guy gives a goofy look like he belongs in a nut house. We all tried it."

"What did you do?"

Maddie tries to imagine the face Billy makes. Walter laughs so hard he spits.

"They gave it to Lyle."

"Hell of a fiddle player."

"Hell yeah."

"You sure look crazy on stage sometimes, Billy."

"That's cuz I'm thinking about Bonnie."

"Bonnie the Blonde."

"I'm going to have some of that. Real soon."

The second night opens with Smokey Montgomery and the Light Crust Doughboys. If anything, it is more crowded than the night before but, without Billy to keep her focused on the stage, Maddie can take in more of her surroundings.

The first thing she realizes is just how big the Riverside Rancho really is. The dance floor is the size of two basketball courts. There is, as she had suspected, a bar. But not just one. *Three* bars staffed by several spiffy looking men pouring drinks and a bunch of gals loading trays with beer mugs. Hidden near the back of the cavernous room is a restaurant and Maddie can smell fried okra and barbequed pork and it makes her smile.

"Sooner?"

Maddie is startled to realize that the girl with the tray is talking to her.

"You're a Sooner, am I right?"

"I was born there," is all Maddie can manage.

"And yer daddy and his daddy before him and so forth and so forth." She was pretty, her hair pulled up in a stylish mass of blonde curls. She sticks out a hand with bright red nails. "Tulsa."

"Maddie." She shakes the girl's hand and then she gets it. "Ratliff City. About 80 miles from Oklahoma City."

"I know folk from Ratliff!" She grabs Maddie's arm and pulls her though the crowd.

The couple turns out to be from Elmore City, about 30 miles from Ratliff but close enough that they take a break from the dance floor to introduce her to Jerry and Penny from Rush Springs who turn out to be related to Maddie on her maternal grandmother's side.

Which leads them to Kitty, who manages the place and might be a second cousin. Kitty exudes maternal love despite her tremendous height. She towers a good two feet over Maddie as she wraps the girl in a bear hug. She'll tell you that her height helps her spot trouble, going all the way back to when she was a little girl, sitting atop the loaded family car, on the look-out for the sheriffs at the California border. These thugs were there to beat back the hordes from the dust bowl with their fists and batons but Kitty and her family made it through. Maddie would later get used to hearing Kitty say, "I got an eye on everything in this club, whether it breathes or it don't." Kitty books the acts at Riverside Rancho, as well as ordering the booze, balancing the books, everything.

As she hugged Maddie on that second night at the Rancho, she said, "dear, you just stick with Kitty, you hear?" There is nothing Maddie would rather do. She feels a warmth and comfort with this group that she hasn't felt in a long time. Talking the same way she talked, sharing experiences and common geography, relaxed intimacy.

A pair of hands catch Tulsa from behind, covering her eyes. "Guess who, Cindy-Loo?"

"Billy Clover!" Tulsa takes his hands and he swings her into a sweeping dance step.

"Got a dance for me, girl?"

Tulsa playfully pushes him away. "I've got work to do. And don't you have a band somewhere around here?"

"Hell yeah," hoots Jerry from Elmore City. "When you going on, cowboy?"

"You going to play 'Cabin in The Hill', Billy?" swoons Penny. "I surely do love that song."

"Thank ya, ma'am. But you best get in line. Bing Crosby loves that number. The Andrew Sisters. Half the crews in this town want to cover it. And you know what? I just might let 'em."

Tulsa pouts. "Don't forget your promise, Big Time. You still haven't taken me for a walk in Ferndell." She turns to Maddie. "That's a little place I know in the park. It's got a quiet little creek and lots of shady trees. Just the place for a boy to take a girl for a long leisurely Sunday stroll. So, when you going to take me, Billy?"

Billy slips his arms around her waist. "*Sooner* than you think." As Tulsa laughs, he asks, "who's your friend?"

"Oh, this is Maddie from back home." Billy smiles and Maddie catches her breath, feeling a warm flush rise on her cheeks. He sticks out his hand.

And he gives her a look.

Maddie's hand freezes midway to Billy's and all the excitement and thrill drains right out of her. The look is haughty. Hungry. Animal. It's in his eyes. It's on his lips.

Tulsa says, "oh, and I never told you. My name is Bonnie."

Billy is under the lights.

"*The creek is a bubbling and the birds a singing, and it sounds like music we know so well, just a boy and girl, holding hands and dancing, beneath the trees down at ol Ferndell.*"

Bonnie shrieks in joy.

Later, walking in the dark woods, Maddie tries to imagine a different BugBear. Not the one from back home, lurking in the cornfields, claws ready to tear apart naughty kids who wander in. The one waiting for someone at the pond to take their clothes off on a dare. The one whose ears perk up when he hears an unheeded call to come in for the evening. Not that BugBear.

An LA BugBear.

What's he like? She imagines he's made up of a bunch of different parts from a bunch of different places. He's young. Maybe still growing but always young. He doesn't have thoughts. Just impulses. If he wants something, he says, "I take it." If he is angry, he says, "I hurt it." But he doesn't have to speak. You can see it in the way his eyes stare, his lips twist.

There is no nuance in his masculinity. The soldier who charges the machine-gun nest, the basketball coach who throws things, the sheriff who doesn't need words because he has a gun—he is the essence of that.

It is a kind of purity. This makes him special—enough to be worshipped. And what better way to be worshipped than with fear.

The LA BugBear. A spoiled boy. A dangerous boy.

"This one's a looker. Ain't she something?"

"You're gonna get these nudies out of here before the wife gets home. You hear me, Billy? All of them.

"Here's one even ol' Sally will like."

"What the hell is this?"

"That's Little Billy. Him and his mom at the beach there at Chickasaw lake."

"Cute."

"Sure, after a quick glance you say that. But take another look. Take a real close look!"

"Don't spill that bottle, Billy."

"You look at it, with one blink of an eye, and all you see is just little me smiling and holding mommy's hand. Look closer at her hand. See how it's clamped so tight. It looks like it's hurting Little Billy. Now look at her jaw—she's angry—she's thinking 'we will get a picture of you at the beach, no matter what!' So, why the hell am I smiling? Any guesses?"

"Not really, Billy..."

"Of course you can't guess! Because you can't see what Billy's seeing. There's a little girl in the parking lot. She is crying, crying like you've never seen, crying like she'll just... pop! And I'm thinking—you can see me thinking right? Well, I am thinking 'what if I could hurt her? Just a little, just enough. Hurt her enough and she'd just do it, just explode!' I'm thinking, 'wouldn't that be a sight to see?'"

"This more of your acting, Billy?"

"Naw. Just a memory."

"Well, keep those memories to yourself. They scare me."

The third night at Riverside Rancho, Kitty has a surprise for Maddie. "We'll call you a typist, but it's more like translating. Nobody has any business trying to make sense out of my scratches and scrawls except a bright girl like you." Maddie has a job.

And Bonnie doesn't show up for work. Her roommate says she never came home the night before.

Billy is a no show as well. Around 11, Tex Williams and his Western Caravan are getting ready to give up. They'd played just about every song they knew when, thankfully, the police raid ends the show.

A dozen men in uniforms with copper buttons block the doors while another dozen march through the crowd, grabbing a guy here and a guy there, lining them up against a wall.

Maddie stands frozen, watching the dark blue line moving steadily towards her.

"You! Girl! Yeah, you!" Walter crouches behind a table, cradling his fiddle like a baby. He holds it towards Maddie, eyes imploring. "You'll see that she gets home safe, won't you?"

Maddie gingerly takes the fiddle. "What do I tell your wife?"

"Tell her I'll be home late." He stands now, facing the approaching cops, resigned. "You know, you're safe, right? Billy's gone home. Gone back to Oklahoma."

A cop motions with a heavy baton, pointing to the wall. Walter dutifully takes his place in the line-up.

"He can't hurt you from way out there," he calls over his shoulder.

Walking home, one thing has changed. But it's changed everything.

She knows she is never going home.

The woods are still dark. And they are still full of the sounds that used to scare her. But now they sound like notes in an unwritten tune—the crack of breaking wood, the rustle of leaves, a whistling wind.

All she has to do is write the melody.

GOLD STAR FOR ROBBIE
by Rob Zabrecky

1984

I'M TRYING TO GET COMFORTABLE IN THE WORLD'S MOST UNCOM-FORTABLE DESK. It's the desk I always sit in during seventh period English at Burroughs High: the one nearest the back door, by the big windows that look out on a few trees and shrubs in the sunny campus courtyard. In front of me are the backs, heads, and shoulders of 30 kids, most of which I can tell you their first and last names, and the streets where they live. That's the thing about growing up in Burbank and going to the same public schools your whole life—you get to know everyone, even by the backs of their heads. They all seem to be paying attention to our teacher, Mr. Johnson, a giant of a man with a voice like an FM DJ, who's on a tear about essay writing. It's kind of trippy: I'm watching them watch him.

The hands on the classroom's clock are dragging around the numbers, moving slower than they ever has. Every few minutes, someone farts and it reeks of day old Pup'N Taco. I'm almost certain it's my elementary school bully, Jonathan Fisk, who sits two desks up and one over from me. He keeps looking around suspiciously every time one is ripped, but I can't be sure it's him. We're on the final stretch until the last bell of the day that I wish was Friday, but is only Tuesday. 15 more minutes.

"Please don't forget to hand in your expository essay tomorrow. 300 to 400 words. It can be about any person, place, or thing that's had an impact on your life," Mr. Johnson says with a tone both bored and scolding, like he's given the assignment 10,000 times.

"You might consider writing about one of the American pioneers or authors who have had schools named after them here in Burbank, like Luther Burbank, Bret Harte, or John Burroughs. You could also write about one of our former Burroughs students who have made names for themselves in show business like Debbie Reynolds. *Singin' in the Rain*, anyone? No? How about Ron Howard, who you probably know as little Opie Taylor from *The Andy Griffith Show* or Richie Cunningham on *Happy Days*. It's your choice. Get creative. Just hand it in at the beginning of class tomorrow."

I understand these guys are all hot shots in their fields, but they also seem like the most boring people known to man.

"You can find information on each of them in the library," he adds.

The last place I'm going to after school is the library. No way.

I look out outside the classroom window at the courtyard, where I'm certain I've locked eyes with a blue jay perched on a nearby tree branch. It's doing this little dance, just for me. As it breaks into a little soft-shoe thing, I feel myself drifting into one of my deep fogs.

Since I can remember, when I lose interest in something or get into a bind, I detach from the real world and drift off to this unknown dreamlike dimension. Sometimes I'm on a merry-go-round at a carnival I've never been to. I'm strapped into one of those carousel horses, being slowly lifted up and down and round and round. Other times I'm peacefully floating alone through outer space, as random memories flash by like shooting stars.

In my deepest of fogs, I've started imagining the courtyard filled with a dozen school kids that look like extras from *Happy Days*. They're sitting in polka-dotted poodle skirts and corny letterman's jackets watching this talented blue jay "puttin' on the Ritz," as they say. The next thing I know the background and kids fade away and the bird's on a nightclub stage. I'm in the audience, watching him from some smoky dive. It's like the scene in *Valley Girl* when the Plimsouls are playing "A Million Miles Away" and I've got my arm around one of the members of Bananarama. Then right in the middle of the guitar solo, just when the bird is really getting into it and everyone's bopping around… BOOM!

I nearly jump out of my chair at the sound of the crash. I suck in a huge breath and look up. There's Mr. Johnson, penetrating my every living fiber with a look of hatred. He must've caught me drifting off and slammed a large stack of books on his desk to regain my attention. I look around and every kid is turned around, looking at me. If anything will get me out of a fog, it's when everyone in class is staring at me. To make things worse, someone just cut one of those awful farts.

"Would you mind joining us, Mr. Zabrecky?!" he demands between his teeth in a Drill Sergeant's condescending baritone. Everyone keeps staring like I'm a two-headed fuck-up. Another fart. This class stinks.

"Would you mind repeating tomorrow's assignment to the class Mr. Zabrecky?"

Lucky for me, I remembered the jist of the assignment before blasting off into my fog.

"300-400 word essay. Due tomorrow."

The bell rings. The tension breaks and the day of school is

over. I'm heading out the door trying to pass by Mr. Johnson's desk unnoticed, but he calls me out.

"Do you really feel like taking this class next semester, Zabrecky?"

"No sir."

"Please pay more attention in class, or you will."

"Understood Mr. Johnson," I say popping on the Ray Bans that were folded up in my jean jacket, jammed next to a half pack of clove cigarettes.

*   *   *

It's not like I hate writing or hate high school. I don't at all. In fact, I'm enjoying my high school experience. It's just that there are so many other things to do and see, and it's damn near impossible to pay attention and catch every word in every class, let alone do homework. But I get it: sometime between now and tomorrow's now I'd better have a paper in my hand. Although my grades average a D+, I don't feel like flunking this class and taking it over next semester.

I throw my books in my locker and make a beeline for the parking lot to see what's happening. The parking lot at my school is actually pretty cool. Monday through Friday, week after week, kids gather around hand-me-down cars on the black tarred lot to listen to MTV music, puff clove cigarettes, goop on eyeliner, and apply last blasts of hairspray before rushing off to class or their afterschool jobs.

I look around and catch eyes with my best bud, Mike Keys, sitting on the hood of his Dodge Dart. It's impossible to miss him because he just dyed his hair bright red. He's exchanging numbers with short skirted cutie Tanya Ellis and her oblong new wavish hair. If you don't know Mike Keys, he's the James Dean of Burbank. We met in elementary school and discovered BMX bikes, skateboards, and music together during our last moments of innocence. Mike Keys—I always call him by his first and last name because it sounds cool—is fearless. Since sixth grade, he has single-handedly showed me how stand up for myself and not to be afraid of kids or authority figures. He's also great looking and girls continuously flock to his olive skin and brown eyes, even in grade school, when he was a model, yes, an *actual* model for the Gemco catalogue. He's kind of a star, at least to me.

These days, he's immersed in a gang called BPO, the Burbank Punk Organization and talks like a Cholo about half the time. He dropped out of school last year after a few altercations with other students and teachers, but hates missing out on anything, so he still drops by to visit the parking lot. Mike Keys is living the ultimate after-school experience.

"Yo ese! There's a new party spot. It's called the Batman Caves. Wanna go?" His voice tells me I'm going whether I want to or not.

I'm between two minds. On one hand, I know I'd better get cracking on that essay. On the other, seeing a place called the Batman Caves is an adventure I can't resist.

"Yeah, let's hit it."

"Cool. You're driving. I'm almost out of gas. But I have this," he says, popping open his truck and removing a six-pack of Miller bottles. "Left over from last weekend. It's warm, but drinkable."

* * *

I should probably mention that I'm on a perfect losing streak of getting fired from after-school jobs. I count four, maybe five, in the past six months. Finding the work has been a breeze, but holding on to any one job or another is a whole different story.

I lost my last job just last week—shrink-wrapping orders for a video duplication company in this desolate part of Burbank, up near Victory and Burbank Blvd. Wavelength Video is owned and run by a heavy-set, disheveled character of a man called Ray Atherton, who produces, and sells all sorts of weird movies on VHS. One of the titles is called *Meatcleaver Massacre*, which Ray is proud to tell you he wrote and produced himself. He also has a catalogue of other weirdo stuff ranging from Charles Manson documentaries to old serial Westerns and TV shows like *Amos & Andy*. Showing up for work an hour late and leaving early didn't cut the mustard for old Ray. I lasted about a month.

"You're a nice kid, Robbie. But I can get a Mexican in here that'll show up on time and do twice the work as you. So long, kid. Good luck. I'm sure you'll be fine," he said, placing my last check in my hand. And that was that.

* * *

We barrel over Barham Blvd in my VW Squareback, on our way to the Batman Caves as a worn-out cassette of Agent Orange's "Living in Darkness" plays at top volume. While we roll onto the famous 101 freeway to Hollywood, Mike Keys, a clove cigarette dangling from his mouth, barks directions,

"Gower! Get off here! Left here! Up here. Keep going till it dead ends."

Within a few minutes we've travelled from one world to the next. We drive up a canyon in the Hollywood Hills, passing all these killer houses that movie stars must live in. It's hard to believe that less than an hour ago I was in English class smelling awful farts and getting the Christ scared out of me by Mr. Johnson. Hollywood is magic. I'm definitely living here someday.

The street ends and I pull into a large empty dirt lot. My VW slides over a bunch of loose rocks, kicking up dust before settling into what feels like a parking spot. Mike Keys grabs the beers and we start up a dirt fire road.

"This way." He stabs out a clove cig on a Smokey the Bear sign. He's always doing cool stuff like that. Like it's no big deal. That's what makes Mike Keys cool. He doesn't even know he's cool.

A short uphill jaunt leads us past some menthol-scented Eucalyptus trees and deserty bushes to a big open space. It looks just like one of those desolate sets from the *Twilight Zone.* We gaze at the base of a steep mountain that has a tunnel leading into darkness. It's quiet and birds are chirping all over the place.

"Welcome to the Batman Caves, ese." says Mike Keys, reaching in the bag and pulling out two warm beers and handing one to me.

I recognize the main cave right away—but *not* as the cave from Batman—it's familiar because I'd just seen it in a Sci Fi 50's flick I'd secretly borrowed from Ray Atherton's place called *Robot Monster.* I'd watched it a couple of days before I was fired, and it's still fresh in my mind. Yep, I'm sure it was shot right here. There's zero chance Mike Keys has seen it, so I keep the thought to myself.

"Right there, dude, the Batmobile comes tearing out of the tunnel at the beginning of the show," he says, like I'm stupid for not seeing it.

"Oh yeah, totally," I say just to agree.

"Heard the caves are haunted by Jim Morrison's ghost. The Doors used to party here, bro. Muy fucking cool. Follow me ese," he says, heading toward the cave.

I nod, pretending I know what he's talking about. I don't. Doesn't sound too far off, though. I bet they did. Above a few desert knolls is the most awesome view of the Hollywood sign I'd ever seen. Seeing it this close I notice that it's in need of a new coat of paint. This place is a perfect romp and change of pace from the streets of Burbank, the Old Zoo, or cruising Mullholland Drive.

Swigging awful tasting warm Miller's, we head into the cave. Once in, it gets dark and cool. It also smells like dried up pee. Deep in the cave, we see that it forks off to a few smaller tunnels. In the distance, at the end of one of them, stands this shirtless kid, gripping a large tree branch like a staff. We gravitate his direction. The sun lights him up and he becomes fully visible. He's got a lean body, long black hair, eyes, and dark skin, and looks like a bum, even though he's too young to be a bum. Maybe he's a dirty hippie Jim Morrison wannabe who just needs a bath. He's got on cut off army pants that are way too big for him, with a necktie as a belt. Whoever he is, he's intense, and staring right at us.

"What are you looking at?" says Mike Keys.

The kid stands there frozen, like a cut-out standee from one of those memorabilia shops on Hollywood Blvd.

"You have a staring problem, bro?' Mike Keys' voice echoes through the cave.

The kid keeps staring. He's really good at just staring. After a few seconds, it gets awkward and Mike Keys makes a move.

"I don't have time for you, clown boy. C'mon Robbie," he says, losing interest in the prospect of fighting the boy. We brush past him and head to the other side of the cave. Outside is another big open space. There's not much to check out, no more caves, outdoor tables, or restrooms. We look back and the kid is nowhere to be found.

We finish chugging the beers and line up the empty bottles on a huge rock. Gathering some golf ball sized rocks, we prepare for a game of bottle break. Mike Keys throws the first rock and hits the bottle right in the center. It explodes and makes a great sound. He's a damn good shot.

"I'm getting into modeling again. I met this chick at the Odyssey on Saturday night who's gonna hook me up with her agent," he says like it's a sure thing, destroying another bottle. I believe him: he looks good in whatever he's wearing, even in the look he's got going right now—jeans and T shirt with a Pendleton tied around his waist. And, since he already modeled for Gemco, he knows how to stand and pose and everything. All he needs to do is dye his hair back to dark brown.

"That sounds cool. I'm gonna start a band and go around the world," I say, knowing I've got a ways to go since I just started playing the electric bass six months ago. I feel a medium sized buzz coming on as I chuck a rock, miss another bottle by a long shot. I'll never be as good of a shot as Mike Keys. No one will.

Mike Keys annihilates five of the six bottles. I got lucky and hit one on my sixth or seventh try. The sun's slipping below a hilly skyline on the west. We're standing around looking at the broken glass when another blue jay—just like the one from class that led me into that deep fog—reminds me of that essay I need to get in tomorrow. It's a buzzkill, but I think about taking that class over again. I've had enough for one day.

"One of us has school tomorrow, and it isn't you. I gotta bail. Just remembered—I got some shit to do."

"Yeah, let's blow this hot dog stand," he agrees.

* * *

A half hour later I drop off Mike Keys at his Dodge Dart in the vacant school parking lot and head home. I mow down a TV dinner, drench two Twinkies with maple syrup and pop them in the microwave for 10 seconds, practically inhaling them with a huge glass of milk and head to my room to get cracking on the essay. I've got Mr. Johnson's voice in my ear, saying we could write about any person or thing. All I know is there's no way I'm writing about John Burroughs, Richie Cunningham or any of those other dull people. I nearly bore myself to death even thinking about them.

Out of left field, I get an idea to write about Jonathan Fisk. I've known him since second grade, when he'd take my lunch money and threaten to kick my ass. I could write about how over the years, he's morphed into this anti-social loner with a large collection of heavy metal T-shirts. Nah. Better not do that in case he somehow reads it and it sets him off to come after me again or something. Besides, he's not even worth writing an essay about. Then Ray Atherton comes to mind. Yeah, Ray: not only does he look like Johnathan Winters' twin brother with less hair, but he's got his own business going and makes movies. Ray's a decent contender. Then Mike Keys comes to mind. He'd be good too. If it weren't for Mike Keys, there's no way I'd be the guy I am now. On second thought I'd better not—I don't want anyone to think I'm gay for Mike Keys or anything. How about that dirty Indian looking kid from the Batman caves? There was something cool about him. I could make up a story about him and nobody would even know if it was true or not.

My buzz has worn off and it's now or never. I kick off my dusty black pointed shoes, flip through some records and settle on Echo & the Bunnymen's new album, *Porcupine*. I roll the vinyl from its record jacket, place Side A on the record player and drop the needle on the first song, "The Cutter." Man, what a killer intro. What an awesome great song. If I could write a song I'd write one just like this.

I perch myself on my bed with a spiral notebook, and find myself drifting off in another fog, catching the vision of Mr. Johnson slamming down those books to get my attention in class, and the commotion it caused. What a weird thing to do to get someone's attention. It's no time to drift off. I put a fresh Bic pen to paper and this comes out:

V-
Good effort

ROBOT MONSTER
ROBBIE ZABRECKY
6TH PERIOD ENGLISH
MARCH 21, 1984

ROBOT MONSTER IS A '50s SCIENCE FICTION
MOVIE ABOUT ALIEN INVASION. THE PROTAGONIST
IS A YOUNG BOY CALLED JOHNNY WHO ALONG
WITH HIS FAMILY ARE THE LAST PEOPLE ON EARTH.
THEY ARE BEING PERSUED BY AN ALIEN CALLED
"RO-MAN" (WHO IS SOME GOON IN A GORILLA COSTUME
AND BIG METAL DIVING HELMET). THE ACTING AND
SPECIAL EFFECTS ARE BAD, IT WAS MADE IN GRIFFITH
PARK. THE BEST THINGS ABOUT THE MOVIE ARE RO-MANS
COSTUME AND THE MUSIC.
RO-MAN'S MISSION IS TO DESTROY ALL HUMAN LIFE.
HE COMMUNICATES AND TAKES ORDERS FROM HIS
LEADER, THE GREAT ONE, WHO BARKS ORDERS THROUGH
A BIG RADIO THAT SPITS BUBBLES. HE'S DONE GREAT,
WIPING OUT HUMANS, EXCEPT FOR JOHNNY AND HIS
FAMILY BECAUSE THEY HAVE AN ANTI-BIOTIC THAT
KEEPS THEM IMMUNE FROM THE ALIEN'S DEATH RAYS
AS RO-MAN IS WORKING ON WIPING OUT JOHNNY AND
HIS FAMILY, HE FALLS IN LOVE WITH JOHNNY'S OLDER
SISTER.
AT THE END OF THE FILM, WE LEARN THAT JOHNNY WAS JUST
DAYDREAMING AND MADE THE WHOLE STORY UP.
IT ENDS WITH US LEARNING THE MOVIE,
WAS JUST A BAD DREAM AND EVERYTHING'S
OKAY - LIKE THE END OF "THE WIZARD OF OZ."

THE MOVIE IS A SOLID REMINDER THAT
SOMETIMES WHEN WE LEAST EXPECT IT,
WE DRIFT OFF AND GO PLACES IN OUR
MINDS THE REST OF THE WORLD CAN'T SEE,
WHICH CAN BE MORE EXCITING THAN THE
WORLD WE LIVE IN. I'M GLAD THE PEOPLE
WHO MADE THIS MOVIE DID BECAUSE
IT'S A GREAT REMINDER THAT SOMETIMES
IMAGINATION RULES OVER REALITY.

HONEY TREE EVIL EYE

1987

"FIRST THING, YOU GOTTA FIND THE DRUMMER," SAYS TROY.

Matt scans the gathering in front of Gazzarri's, two dozen guys pushing fliers at anyone passing by the club on the Sunset Strip .

"These guys are all varying degrees of cocky and desperate. The equation we are looking for is most parts desperation." Troy nods triumphantly. "And there he is!"

Matt studies the dude. Nothing immediately makes him stand out. His hair might be less teased than most, his nylons more torn. Like many of the others, he is wearing an article of clothing (here a headband) sporting the name of a band he admires/has seen in concert (Scorpions) and an article with the name of his own band (t-shirt) (Blast Zone.)

The dude senses their attention and swaggers over. "This is gonna be a massive show!"

The billboard reads "MotorCycle Boy", which is why Matt and Troy are here. Below this top-biller are listed the following bands in descending order, and smaller type size. Felon. Hydrogen. Skid Marks. Blast Zone.

"You do not want to miss it! My band is going to tear that stage apart! Let me set you up."

"Well…" Troy pauses.

After a beat, the dude gets it. "Stevie."

"Well, Stevie. I understand that, here at Gazzarri's, all the bands have the hottest guys playing the hottest music." Troy continues quoting the TV ad. "If the guys ain't hot and they ain't playing the hottest music, they don't get on my stage. And by 'my,' I mean Bill Gazzarri, the Godfather of Rock n Roll."

"I don't know about those scags in Felon." Stevie nods gravely towards a group of rockers sporting matching Bride of Frankenstein streaks, "but Blast Zone is next level. We rock. Hard!"

He plays some drums in the air around him. Troy is right. Desperate. Matt is glad he'd been the one who scored the mushrooms, not the tickets.

"I got you covered. I'm in the band, I can get you a deal."

Stevie then makes a mistake by taking a breath before launching into the rest of his sales pitch. Troy cuts him off. "Let's do the math. Opening spot on a Friday night costs you about $800? Right?"

"Uh…"

"Let's say $800. Tickets at the door are $20. At that rate, you need to sell 40 tickets to cover the front money to the promoter. But who is going to pay you full price when they can take a little walk to the ticket counter and pay that much. So, $15 and it's like 60 tix now." He stares pointedly at the stack of tickets in Stevie's hand. "Looks like you've got a long way to go."

Troy holds up two $10 bills. "Two please."

Stevie swaps tickets for money. "Be sure to get here early. We go on at seven."

Troy's self-satisfied look dissolves a bit as Stevie rushes back to his bandmates, triumphantly waving the cash.

The pair strolls down the strip. With their shoulder-length

hair and pleather jackets, they do, and don't, blend in. It's the result of a carefully examined calculation. They pass the Roxy. It's a wild scene. Guys unload equipment emblazoned with band names. "Prime Suspects." "Ferrari." "Narcissus." Fliers are stapled to telephone poles, layered on walls, pasted to construction facades, phone booths. "Rebel With A Cause." "Vixen." "Tuff."

"We got three hours until Motorcycle Boy. You still wanna drop at the Hollywood sign?"

"And miss Blast Zone?!"

Matt is happy to get a laugh. He feels like he needs a win after Troy's bravado performance.

"How about this?" He rips a flier from a passing pole, brandishing it. "Feel like getting your Inner Hippie on?"

The flier reads "Love In. Sunset. Griffith Park by the Carousel. All gentle souls welcome."

"Is it still the Summer of Love?"

"I think it's the technically the Fall of Love now, but definitely still the Age of Aquarius."

Matt and Troy don't know each other very well. They met last month in the writer's room for season 3 of *Riptide*. Each of them is "the new guy" and they need to be friends or enemies. The head writer keeps saying they think alike. Who knows if that's true, but he's right this time.

As they head towards Griffith Park, each of them is thinking, "Oh man, this is going to be fun!"

The Griffith Park Carousel. These guys could tell you that it inspired the carousel Walt Disney built in his park, in Fantasyland, on the other side of Sleeping Beauty's Castle from Main Street, USA. Main Street was, in turn, modeled after the small town of Marceline, Missouri, where his family lived for several years when he was a child. They could also tell you that Disney was miserable when he lived there, and thus his nostalgia for the place seems misplaced, and his monument to it bizarre.

They could tell you that and more, but they are busy scanning the sloping grass below—the picnicking Hispanic families, the toddlers negotiating a final ride on the carousel, old men in straw hats pushing carts and hawking melting ice cream, old women cooking bacon-wrapped hot dogs, an impromptu Ultimate Frisbee game...

And a woman with flowers in her hair laying out blankets on the grass.

Troy is dubious. "Someone's got *Great Expectations*."

Matt dutifully hums the chorus of KISS' 1976 album-filler by that name, but he's nervous. This lone hippy is underwhelming, and Matt knows that this was his idea.

The strum of a distant guitar signals the cavalry has arrived. Descending from the parking lot comes a hairy guy wearing a jeans vest over his naked chest and strumming an acoustic guitar. He leads a rag-tag band of merry pranksters. And, yes, they are prancing.

The boys beam. "3-2-1. Drop!" They simultaneously swallow a handful of mushrooms. As the arriving cavalcade launches an avalanche of hugs, Troy and Matt settle in on a picnic table with a grand view of the merriment below.

"Shall we review the history of the Love-In, my friend and colleague, Matthew Pepperstone?"

"Indeed, Dr. Hanson. Regale me."

"While it is universally believed that the Love-In originated in San Francisco in 1968 with the hippies gathering in Golden Gate Park for days of drugs and music, the first Love-in may have been held in 1967, in Elysian Park, not far from in here. Near Dodger Stadium."

The boys both raise their middle fingers in the direction of San Francisco.

"It was a Moody Blues concert, if I'm correct."

"A cancelled Moody Blues concert." Troy corrected. "They held a spontaneous free concert in a field across from the stadium that lasted two days. Imagine fans leaving the ball park after some good old American baseball and running into a thousand half-naked long-hairs. What a crazy mismatch."

Matt considered the Hispanic families peppering the park around the small circle of hippies. "Not too hard to imagine."

The hippies all join hands and make a circle, swaying back and forth, back and forth.

"Does anyone remember la-ughter?" Troy shouts, quoting the Led Zeppelin concert film, *The Song Remains The Same.*

Matt cheers, quoting the band's reaction. He riffs, adding, "I do! I do! I remember laughter, Mr. Plant!"

So far the 'shrooms are more speedy than trippy but that's okay. These guys like to talk.

"You know what we need in this scene? We need a hackey sack."

On cue, one appears, and a group peels off from the rest, heads down, kicking, and jumping, crying out in joy.

"Whoa. I'm magic."

A cheer goes up as the Green Tortoise parks on the tennis court, vomiting out a dozen weary hippies that have sat on the floor of this re-purposed school bus all the way from San Francisco. The shocks are shot and there are no bathrooms but it's only $50 and all kinds of smoking is allowed. And it's painted green.

"Whoa." Troy is impressed. "This is 'shaping up nicely.'"

Matt picks up the thread, mocking their head writer. "'Quite nicely. Quite nicely, indeed.'"

"Stephen is going to be very happy." Matt faux crosses himself, evoking the name of Stephen Cannell, creator of *Riptide* and their boss. The man is on a decade long winning streak—Barretta, Rockford Files, Baa Baa Black Sheep, The Greatest American Hero, The A-team. He owns it all, including the 12 story building on La Brea where they work.

"We've got a dynamite beginning." Matt laughs but Troy cuts him off. "No, really! We've got a dynamite beginning."

"Fade up...."

"Exterior Park. Dusk. As the sun slowly descends over the carousel, a group of flower children arrive, like a people lost out of time..."

"Dissolve to..."

"Park. Later. The crowd has grown." He studies the Gathering. "There's a guy on stilts. Another dressed as a medieval jester. The din of a dozen tambourines. Troy's eyes drift to the parking lot above the carousel. "Right on time. It's our Second Act escalation."

Horn blares, a tricked-out van bounces into the lot. Speakers on the top pump out party tunes.

"My girl wants to party all the time, party all the time, party all the time!"

The van does a celebratory spin around the lot, wheels squealing. The wildly colorful paint job on its side reads "Budweiser!" and "The King of Beers!"

The music kicks into high gear as the van's doors slide open and out jump the Bud Light Girls. Six models in red-white-and-blue one-piece swimsuits.

"R-O-C-K in the USA! R-O-C-K in the USA!"

Low-riders leave their cherry cars. Picnickers join them. The girls toss Bud Light t-shirts, Bud Light beer cozies.

Over the speaker booms an excited voice. "Here he is! The dog you've been waiting for! One happenin' Dude! The Original Party Animal! Spuds MacKenzie!"

Sure enough, Spuds leaps out and is swarmed by the adoring girls. It's a costume but it's all there. The white fur, the pointed ears, the long snout. He whips off some dark shades to reveal the signature black circle around his left eye.

"Go Spuds! Go Spuds Go!"

Of course, Troy and Matt know a lot about Spuds. How his debut commercial during the Super Bowl launched a massive ad campaign. All the crazy commercials that followed—Spuds cooling it on the beach, Spuds playing drums at a Texas BBQ, Spuds in a tuxedo behind a grand piano, Spuds in a hot tub always surrounded by hot and adoring girls.

The guys dig that he's become an unexpected populist outlaw hero fighting for the rights of Free Speech and Partyin'. Mothers Against Drunk Driving has launched boycotts. Strom Thurmond jumped on the bandwagon, banning Spuds from his congressional district. The State of Ohio even sought legal action after he showed up at a mall dressed as Santa.

The dog's real name is Honey Tree Evil Eye. And he is a she.

Troy looks a little pale. He tries to pick up the game again. "Do we have a strong role for Perry?" *Riptide* co-star Perry King often complains that, out of the three detectives living on the boat in the Redondo Beach Marina, he hardly ever plays the lead role. He has even suggested that RoBoz, the team's robot helper, gets bigger parts. He isn't wrong. The writers hate him and his pretty boy moustache.

The Bull Terrier party going down in the parking lot is mainly ignored by The Gathering. Except for one guy, who proudly stands at the edge of the lot in a Bob Marley t-shirt, his middle-finger raised in silent protest of the corporate canine revelry.

Spuds poses for pictures, either unaware or unfazed.

Out of nowhere, Troy takes a hard right turn. "None of this distracts from the ridiculousness of a Love-In in 1987! In fact, *in fact!*, it reveals it! It underlines it!" His eyes are wide—pupils big black spots.

"Look around! There's everything right here that you'd need for an incredible, I don't know, essay, no, an *article* in Harpers! About the collision of two forms of inauthenticity."

Matt watches him chase his words, spinning out of control.

"But...but... was any of this ever authentic? How is this Gathering less authentic than the Golden Gate Love-ins? Or Woodstock?" His jaw works as he thinks it through. "Sure, these guys here are mimicking the behavior and fashion from the Sixties, but weren't the "original" hippies just taking their cues from other Bohemian cultures? So, the question is, what's the barometer? Is it 'who's first?' Is it 'who's biggest?' And the bigger question is *who decides*?!"

A beat and then Matt bursts out laughing. Not appreciative "you're blowing my mind here, Troy" laughter. A mocking laugh. A mean laugh. A hard laugh right in Troy's face.

Troy struggles. "I mean...I guess, I mean..."

"ImeanImeanImean!" Matt stutters. Troy sags.

Matt preens, reveling in his newly attained Alpha role. He shows off his verbal agility. *He's* not too high to rattle off a high-speed list of a half-dozen synonyms for "hippie." (Freak, yippie, digger, tripper, drop out, acid head.) He fills in info that Troy neglected in his discourse on the Elysian Park Love-In - most notably that when the police raided the field after two days, they hauled off over a ton of trash and had to quarantine the area for a month because of all the piss and shit.

As Troy sinks deeper into his funk, Matt rises. He plays a little word game, rearranging letters in Troy's name for hilarious results, including "They Snnore." He recites from memory the lyrics to Spud's Beach Boys inspired theme song.

"Well, there's a super party animal, his name is Spuds Mackenzie, with a beach in sight, and a cold Bud Light, he's in a party frenzy..."

The sun is setting. In the parking lot, the van is packing up. Discarded Bud Light coupons flutter across the concrete.

It all suddenly seems very sad to Matt. Very sad. Soul-crushingly sad. He pictures himself getting a Bud Light girl to take a photo of him with Spuds. In the photo, he's got an arm around Spud's shoulder, pointing at him with a big smirk on his face.

Matt remembers other such photos. Him on Santa's lap, pointing at Old Nick and smirking. At his brother's college graduation, pointing at the diploma and smirking. Pointing at a vomiting friend. A girlfriend's painful sunburn. A misspelled road sign. The Virgin Mary. Smirking.

The image of his smirking face rises above him like a giant balloon. He looks older now. Everything else is gone. He's been transformed into one gigantic smirk.

"Hey Spuds. Where you going?" the blond Bud Girl shouts.

Spuds is walking away from the van.

"Spuds?"

He doesn't stop. The girls confer for a moment. The van drives off.

He wanders down the hill, passing Matt and Troy at their table. They wordlessly watch him go.

Paws clasped above his head like a victorious prizefighter, Spuds wades into The Gathering. He high-fives reluctant hippies. Pogoes around the circle. Grabs a passing reefer and pretends to take a drag and pass out.

The pair is absorbed.

"What is he doing?"

"He's…crashing the party…"

Spuds grabs a guitar and boogies to "Hound Dog." He juggles tambourines.

The medieval joker steps up to him, groovy but firm voice. "Hey man, this is sort of *our* scene, you dig?"

Spuds flashes him a peace sign and takes his arms, jumping up and down, leading this self-proclaimed leader in a bouncy dance.

The guys just stare.

It's dark now and Troy and Matt stumble around the site of the old zoo, a short walk from the carousel. They pass the abandoned cages. The graffiti-covered stone walls. Yes, there is an interesting history here, but these guys are beyond that.

Stray observations slip through their heads…this is where the Mentors' shot the cover of *Up The Dose*… the band's members names include Sickie Wifebeater, Papa Sneaky Sperm Shooter… Tipper Gore really hated that band…

But nothing catches hold. Just water passing over smooth stones.

They just wander. No more words.

SCOOP OF THE CENTURY

1999

Stan found working the concession stand tedious. Before that, he'd worked in the pro-shop, which was better, but he'd still describe it as tiresome. Before that, he'd been a caddie, which hadn't been a bore, but it was a lot of work.

All in all, he'd been working at the Wilson and Harding golf course in Griffith Park for nearly fifty years.

The only fun, really, had been selling his stories. In the fifties, it had been innocent stuff for the gossip rags. Stuff like who-was-dating-who—stuff he overhead golfers chatting about on the links. He'd get a couple bucks from the reporters in the bar for a few well-remembered tid-bits. As the swinging sixties and seventies came around, drugs were a big seller. His man at the Times moved to the tell-all rags and his lust for a good drug and sex scoop was insatiable. That was when Stan bought the Pontiac Firebird. Not bad for a guy who barely finished third grade.

Then, for a long time, it was so-and-so was gay, so-and-so was a lesbian, and Stan didn't like that stuff too much, but, by then, he was really hooked on the game.

Along came the tabloids and his contacts started to dry up. And then, the thing that nearly killed the whole deal, he almost got caught. "LEE MAJORS CHEATS ON FARRAH" made him a pretty penny. Problem was that, not only was it not true, but somehow the gossip around the club turned on *him*. He'd blabbed. He was a rat. He was dirt.

Besides, the course took a dive, celebrity-wise. Not much dish left to dish.

So Stan laid low for a good decade. Probably closer to two.

Now…the concession stand. Soft drinks for the tee-totalers. Bags of chips for the losers too cheap for the clubhouse restaurant. Tedious. He'd been trying to sell the Haunted Park thing for years. He brought it out of mothballs.

The jist was this. Griffith J. Griffith was the namesake of the park. They could get a good picture of the statue near Los Feliz. Griffith wanted to give the city of Los Angeles the land for the park—a lot of fucking land—and all the money to build the Observatory and the Greek Theater. For free. But the City wouldn't take it.

Why? Cuz he was a shitty drunk. He was a shitty drunk when he got to LA and started calling himself "Colonel." He was a shitty drunk when he had the peacock ranch in Griffith Park and sold feathers for the latest hat craze and tickets to see a live peacock up close. And when he did all the other crazy schemes that got him rich? He was a shitty drunk then as well.

How shitty? When he was 53, he shot his wife in the eye and tossed her out a second floor window of a hotel in Santa Monica. Salacious, right? And paid his lawyers so much that he got off with two years in San Quentin. Injustice, right?

Who would want a giant park in the middle of their city named after this asshole? Not Los Angeles.

Okay, they ultimately agreed to take the land and the money but long after Griffith J. Griffith was dead. And here's where the "haunted" part came in. Apparently, his ghost walks the grounds of the golf course in the middle of Griffith Park at night. Apparently, a long-time employee has seen this ghostly visage several times over his many years at Wilson and Harding and heard it wail, "This park is mine. This park is mine" many many times.

Tabloid gold, right?

Nada. Not a nibble.

Until, the afternoon of Tuesday, April 13th, 1999.

Stan was on his way to the parking lot when he saw OJ Simpson putting his clubs in the trunk of his car. No big deal— OJ was always playing the public parks since his rich friends booted him from the fancy courses in Beverly Hills and Bel Air. Though he'd been acquitted, no one believed he was innocent, and no one wanted him in their clubhouses. Except places like Wilson and Harding where no one gave a shit.

Stan's old Pontiac stalled at the exit and OJ banged on the window. OJ was sweating and talking fast. OJ said that a guy had just pulled a gun on him. OJ told the guy, "take my wallet, take my car, take everything." But the guy said "I'm not here for the car. I'm here for you." Thinking fast, OJ bit the guy's hand. The guy dropped the gun and took off out of the lot in a white van.

Stan moved his car and OJ took off in hot pursuit.

When he got home that night, he went straight to his book-shelf and found his thesaurus. He looked up "haunted" and found a synonym: "cursed."

Then he knew he had a story.

SOLO

1990

JASON PARKED THE CAR IN A TURN-OFF. Not exactly hidden but not in plain sight. He helped Bea out of the back, careful to make sure she didn't bump her grey-haired head on the door frame.

"This way." Jason pointed his cane towards a faint path between sage scrub and walnut trees. Bea smiled and put her bony hand in his. He withdrew it.

They began to walk.

He'd heard a story about Griffith Park. About a couple that was making out on an isolated picnic table when lightning struck a nearby tree, which fell, crushing the lovers. There was a second part about a ranger that went to fix the table years later and was run off by a ghost. Hikers took pictures of the crushed picnic table and posted them online. People wrote about their own supernatural experiences at the site.

It had taken Jason just over a minute online to prove to himself that it was all junk. He found the first telling of the story. Posted on April Fools' Day. With a disclaimer at the beginning stating that nothing that followed was true, just a fun story the writer made up. And another disclaimer at the end. Repeating the same message. "I made this up. It's all fake."

There was another story that he never tried to disprove. The story of the feral boy who lived in Griffith Park and devoured the unlucky ones that wandered off the path.

It was a couple hours still from sundown. Jason lead Bea up a slight slope, headed towards the more remote part of the park.

He'd never been good at this. Goodbyes. Break-ups. Moving on. Changing course. A new start. All that shit.

He'd been a songwriter in his youth. More importantly, he had been a part of a songwriting team. One-half of that team. Partners.

They'd had some luck. This was in the late 70s. Sold some songs to some of the bigger pop stars. Three minor hits got lots of airplay. A couple of producers considered them "go to guys". A breakfast cereal jingle when times were lean.

Arthur, that was his partner, got sick. Cancer. Only thirty-two. Of course, Jason stuck by him. When the writing sessions got shorter and more infrequent. When they had to give up their monthly spot at McCabe's where they workshopped their new stuff. When their manager dropped them.

Until Arthur died.

"On My Own" came singing its way into his mind. He didn't write that one. Burt Bacharach and Carole Bayer Sager did. In fact, he only started writing again after Arthur died. When the residuals stopped coming. When no one remembered him. If only he hadn't been so afraid to go out on his own.

The sun was hot. It seemed to get hotter as the woods got denser. He pressed on, beating branches out of his way with the cane. Bea followed, silently.

He would learn his lesson this time. He laughed. He already had. Once before.

Ten years ago, he took his head out of the sand. He looked

hard at his life and at Bea. After all their time together, things had become lifeless and dreadful. Old wounds never seemed to heal. They were living a life of tiptoeing around landmines for weeks or months or years before stomping on each and every one they could find. Exploding. Breaking things. Then retreating back into the unbearable routine.

This time, he acted. He looked up an old flame. They dated. Looked for an apartment.

Then, Bea got sick. Twice in a lifetime!

The Alzheimer's came on fast, and the decline was swift.

How could he leave her? At a time like this? There had been love there once. Hadn't twenty years meant at least this much? That he would stay with her, put his head down and hold her hand through these bad, final years.

The kicker? The dementia changed her. Her worry lines seemed to disappear. Her smile got bigger and came easier. The dark, brooding, ever-watchful eyes got calm, often wide with wonder, or soft with happy memories. Sometimes she was so sweet, like they had never experienced any pain. It was torture.

And she didn't die. And didn't die.

So, no, he didn't research the story of the boy. He didn't go to Snopes. He didn't google "boy in griffith park fake." He chose to believe.

Bea was ahead of him now, strolling happily into the ever thicker sycamores. Soon she'd be surrounded.

He turned then and walked swiftly away.

For a while, he rushed. Breathing hard. Hurrying over the rough ground. Soon he was far away. He slowed.

He could move on now. The old flame wasn't a possibility—that time had passed. But something would happen. Something *could* happen.

The path back to the car was difficult to find, full of false turns and dead ends, but he felt like he was getting close when he heard the drums.

The image that immediately jumped into his mind was from King Kong. The natives beating the drums, opening the giant gate, welcoming the monstrous ape to devour the bound beauty. The helpless sacrifice screaming and fighting her constraints, but there's no escape.

He was running now. Towards the sound of the drums.

He bashed his way through the jagged chaparral, tearing his clothes, cutting his hands, his face. He broke out into an open space.

He almost laughed. It was absurd.

In the middle of the clearing sat a drum kit. Not just a drum or two. Bass kick drum, toms, floor toms, high hats, snares, cymbals. A solid circle of jet black and gleaming chrome.

A young guy—dyed-dark hair with streaks, kamikaze head band, ripped jeans vest—was using every piece. Wailing on them.

His van was parked a hundred yards away at the side of the road. Jason could picture the whole thing. Practice rooms are expensive. Roommates complain. There's lots of empty space in the park. Why not.

The dude's hair flew. His sweat flew. He whirled and pointed his sticks at an arena full of screaming fans.

He had an audience of one. Bea's hands were raised high above her head. They waved back and forth as she rocked side to side. Head thrown back, smiling at the heavens. Her feet shuffling to the beat.

The drummer slowed it down. 1-2. 1-2. 1-2. Fill.

"Oh! Yeah!" shouted Stevie, which was the drummer's name, between heavy bass drum beats. 1-2. 1-2. 1-2.

"Oh! Yeah!" echoed Bea.

Stevie's sticks travelled across the drums, producing a thrilling, if intrinsically corny, cavalcade of tappedity-tap.

"Oh! No!" 1-2. 1-2. 1-2.

"Oh! No!" Tappedity tappedity tap.

"One more for all you lovers out there!" Stevie pointed at the cheap seats and cupped an ear. "Oh! Yes!"

"Oh! Yes!"

"Let me hear you, Griffith Park!"

Jason roared with the rest of the imaginary lovers.

CAROUSEL
by Patrick Cooper

1992

"I CAN'T REMEMBER THE COLOR OF HIS HAIR," WALTER SAID AND HAILEY STARTED CRYING.

"Don't," she said. "Please don't."

"Last night, I saw him again. Damndest thing. Only I can't remember the color of his hair."

Hailey collected herself and said, "There's a guided walk at the park later today." She switched off the coffee machine. "It starts at the observatory and goes up to Berlin Forest. I know you say you're not ready, but if we wait any longer we may blow this whole thing. We'll go when I get back from work."

Walter put his forehead down on the kitchen table. It was his way of dodging.

"I can't do this on my own, Walt. People ask questions. I can't keep this up much longer. We need to fix this."

Walter bit the inside of his cheek. He could hear cars go by out on the street. The squeal of bus brakes. People shuffling on and off. If he went out there, they'd know. Everybody would know. They'd be able to read it on his face in big, bold print like a children's book.

Hailey said, "No one will know. You'll be with me and they'll see us together and we'll be just like any other couple. Just like any other couple, Walt."

Walter looked through the kitchen window at the sycamore tree. Maybe she was right.

* * *

Around 4:30am. That's the time that haunted Walter Nichols. The time his heart used to jolt him awake during his drinking days. He figured it was his body hitting that first anxious wall of withdrawal. Doing the ol' gin jitterbug. All he could do was lie there next to Hailey and try not to tremor so bad that it woke her up.

He could turn on his side and watch the sun come up through the window. Or turn the other way and enjoy the sight of his wife's dark hair resting softly on the pillow. Just stay in bed until she left for work and he could start drinking again.

Walter put the bottle down six months ago and took to sleeping pills - Halcion. Hailey insisted. The pills didn't lead to a better night's sleep though, because now the intruder accompanied the 4:30am jolt. His heart would kick and he'd wake up, rigid and aware. His eyes would focus on Hailey's dark hair, but it felt like he was using another pair of eyes. Ones that could see in another part of the room where the intruder was standing, watching him.

Sometimes he'd hear his approach first. Little feet on the hardwood of the hallway that would turn silent when they hit the bedroom's carpet. Other times the intruder would already be in the doorway.

It took Walter a few days to build up the courage to turn over and look at him. He knew who it was and Walter feared that the sight of the intruder would either be an unearned comfort to him or drive him insane.

The first time Walter turned and looked in the doorway, it

wasn't comfort or insanity that came to him. Walter Nichols felt only a sour pressure behind his eyes as he tried to remember his hair color.

"No, that can't be right," he said and mashed his palms into his eyes until it hurt.

* * *

Walter tilted his head back and closed his eyes. He knew he looked corny standing like that. Like some convict freshly sprung, soaking in the outside world after a hefty stretch. But hell, that's how he felt.

"Look at you," Hailey said, nudging his shoulder. "Is that a smile?"

Walter looked at his wife and the past six months melted away for a moment. "It just feels good being outside. You were right about that."

"Of course I was." They kissed and she hooked her arm in his and they walked on.

Griffith Park was buzzing with a peculiar energy that evening. Couples were walking hand in hand. People jogged the paths. Parents watched their kids bob up and down on the carousel. Some old timers fed the birds. But looming over the scenery was tension about the oncoming verdict.

Walter and Hailey Nichols hadn't been following the trial. His funk had been so low that some days she had to remind him to eat, to take his pills. And Hailey was too busy sustaining their delicate fictional bubble to watch the news.

"I'm going to the restroom," she said. "Hang tight?"

"I'll hang right here," Walter said, nodding at the carousel.

Hailey smiled and walked away. The carousel's organ kicked into an upbeat waltz. Walter watched the jewel-encrusted horses make their rounds. About a dozen kids were taking a ride. Either hooting and waving at their parents or looking miserable. There were no in-betweens.

Walter's eye caught a glimpse of black hair turn the corner around the back end of the carousel. His stomach knotted.

"Hold up," Walter said to himself. "Hold up a second." He looked over to the left, waiting for the carousel to swing the kid back into sight. "C'mon…c'mon." Were the horses always this slow?

There he was. The black haired kid. Black as the hoof of the horse he was riding.

"Son of a bitch. Russ?" Walter stepped towards the carousel. The kid's horse turned the corner again. Walter waited. His heartbeat echoed in his ears. The carousel went around twice more. The kid was gone.

Parents grabbed their kids off the carousel and hustled away. There was commotion all around Walter now. He made his way to the carousel operator.

"Did they all get off?" he asked the hollow-eyed youth.

"They're off, man," the operator said pointing to a small radio he'd been listening to. "All of em. The lot of em. Not guilty. The scumbags."

"What?" Walter said. "No, did a kid stay on the carousel? Where's the one with the black hair?"

The operator tucked the radio under his arm and locked the carousel controls. He said, "Black hair? I'm outta here before shit gets hairy downtown. I suggest you do the same." He excused himself and took off in a half-jog.

Walter looked around. Everyone seemed to be hurrying away. Darting back to their cars. A few parents were physically dragging their kids, kicking up dust. In the distance, sirens.

Walter ran to the other side of the carousel, searching in between the horses. He found nothing but a shoelace and some candy wrappers.

"But that was his hair color," he said to himself. He scratched the back of his head and suddenly felt afraid.

From a cluster of trees behind him, Walter heard a sob. He turned and saw a little boy with dark hair smacking bark and crying.

"Hey!" Walter said. "There you are."

The boy looked at Walter. His freckled cheeks turned down in a grimace and he said, "I know what you did." The voice wasn't a kid's at all. It was guttural, deliberate. "I know what you did and I'm gonna tell."

Walter gasped. The world spun and his knees gave out. Hailey caught him from behind.

"Walter!" she said. "Honey, what's wrong? I was looking for you. We need to go. People said it's going to get bad…"

"Russ!" he said, steadying himself on his feet. He grabbed her shoulders and pointed. "He knows."

Hailey looked over and damned if her knees didn't almost give out too. Same size, same hair, even the dimple on his chin. Christ. The freckles weren't right, but they'd be keeping him out of the sun anyway and maybe they'd fade away in time.

She shrugged out of Walter's grip and nearly tripped making her way over to the kid. "Hey there," she said and crouched down in front of him. Her eyes scanned over his features. "Are you okay?"

"Not supposed to talk to strangers," the boy said, looking at the tree, not her.

Walter heard this. It was the normal voice of a young boy. But it wasn't a second ago. He knew.

"We're not strangers, honey," Hailey said. "Me and my husband, that's Walter, we're friends of your parents. And they had to run but they asked us to take you home."

"I can't find them," the boy said.

"We know. They had to run. We'll take you home."

"Where did they go?"

"There's trouble coming and they had to run. Now we better hurry too, before the trouble gets us."

"What trouble?"

Hailey stroked the boy's dark hair. "Your parents always call you sweetheart when they talk to us. They call you that so much I always forget your real name. What is it again?"

"Eric. What's the trouble? Where are they?"

Hailey smiled and took Eric's hand. He winced.

* * *

Walter stared at the boy across the kitchen table. The hair color was right, he was sure of that now.

"Well, I talked to the police," Hailey said, putting the phone back on the wall receiver. "They said they talked to your parents and the way things are right now, it's best if you just stay with us until things quiet down. Chaos, is the word they used. They said downtown is chaos. Do you know what that word means, Eric? Chaos?"

Behind the glass of milk he was chugging down, Eric shook his head.

"It's bad." Hailey pulled up a chair next to Eric and rubbed his back. "It's very, very bad."

Eric wiped away the milk mustache and said, "Did they say how long it would be very, very bad?"

"No, but it could be for a while. Now finish your milk and we'll get you in the bath."

"This milk tastes funny."

Hailey continued rubbing his back. She looked over his shoulder. Made sure he finished the drink. The residue of the sleeping pill clung to the bottom of the glass. She had only put one in the drink, unlike Walter's usual dose of six.

Walter watched Eric drink the milk. It is the same hair color. Not the hair of the intruder. He smacked the table. Eric and Hailey jumped. The milk glass vibrated.

Walter pointed at Eric. "See that, Hail," he said. "See that?"

"Walter, honey," Hailey's eyes were wide now. She said the word slowly. "Don't."

"Maybe I didn't hit him. Not if he's right there. You told me I did, but maybe I didn't."

Eric shrank back in his chair, scared. Hailey got up and said, "You had a long day, hon. You should get some rest." She moved to the counter above the sink and got the bottle of Halcion. "I can handle little Eric for the rest of the night."

Walter rubbed his palms over his eyes. Was he tired? No. Maybe just a bit groggy. "I think," he started to say. Then he looked at Eric. The hair color was right. But if he saw the intruder again, he could be sure. "I think you're right. I'm wiped." He smacked the table again for emphasis. "I'm wiped and I'd like to go to bed now."

Hailey shook three pills out of the bottle.

* * *

4:30am. The jolt. The firm awareness. Walter stayed on his side, facing the back of Hailey's head. She had stayed up late watching L.A. burn on TV. Walter waited but the intruder never showed up.

He rolled over and looked in the doorway. There was no one there. Walter slowly kicked the sheets off. He sat up and got out of bed, careful not to wake Hailey. He looked down at her, waiting a minute to see if she'd stir. Then he went into the hallway and opened the door to his son's room.

The baseball nightlight gave the room a dreamy glow. Walter laughed, remembering how he had told Hailey that was his biggest fear: that his son wouldn't like baseball. Like a lot of things he said when he drank, that was a lie. His biggest fear was that somehow he'd kill his son.

He walked slow over to the bed and looked down at Eric—the Dodgers comforter pulled all the way up to that mess of black hair. He hesitated for a moment then took a seat on the bed.

That really was his biggest fear. Killing his son. Not intentionally, of course. By some accident or neglect or something worse. But the way the universe kept dealing him a bum hand, Walter feared the worse all of the time. It started with the layoffs at Boeing. He was one of tens of thousands over at the Downey plant who'd been given the boot. Not that he particularly liked being an assembly technician, but it made him feel useful. Every time a plane flew overhead, Russ would point and cheer.

Resentment and selfishness and boredom drove him to the bottle. At least he got to stay home with his son, he would tell himself. He wouldn't have to miss a second of him growing up. Not a lot of parents could say that.

* * *

That unseasonably cold afternoon last October, they decided

to play hide and seek. Walter agreed to let his son hunt first. Walter was five gins deep at this point, so he was feeling very agreeable.

While Russ counted in the backyard under the sycamore, Walter scurried along the side of the house and ducked behind a hedge. At the count of 30, his son started searching. First in the kitchen, where daddy kept the bottles above the fridge. That was his first instinct. Check there. Then the couch, where daddy slept most nights.

Around the two-minute mark Walter got impatient. He was itching for another pull and started restlessly bopping up and down behind the hedge. Through the living room window, his son saw the top of his head. He ran outside and caught his dad there behind the hedge.

"Dammit, what gave me away?" Walter said, messing up Russ' hair.

"You were doing the jitterbug, dad!" his son said, laughing. "Like this!" He shook his head and jumped up and down.

They both laughed. Walter laughed until it hurt. Christ, his son was a card. Always doing impressions.

It was Walter's turn to count under the sycamore. His count to 30 lasted a little longer because he started thinking about what time it was. Thinking that maybe Hailey would come home soon and ruin their fun.

Walter looked for his son in the usual spots—places he'd found him before. He didn't find him under the bed or in the closet, and after combing the backyard, he ran out of ideas. Figured he'd check in the kitchen again.

One, two more pulls from the bottle of gin and Walter forgot they were playing hide and seek all together. His pickled brain wasn't letting him think about anything but how he'd be out of booze soon. Shit, look at the clock. Hailey would be on her way home any minute. Tick tock. She wouldn't let him drive in this condition to get more. And she sure as hell wouldn't go out for him. Tick tock.

Before he backed out of the driveway, a thought scratched its way to the front of Walter's brain. A game. You were playing a game and it isn't over yet. You're supposed to find something. He shook it from his mind and threw the car in reverse.

He saw the trash can in the rearview mirror a second before running it over completely.

* * *

Walter looked down at Eric and thought, "He's here. He's really here. And now things can get back to normal." He smiled and was about to go back to bed when Eric stirred.

The Dodgers comforter shifted down, revealing Eric's face. His eyes flickered open and looked up at Walter. He cringed and tried to roll away from him, but Walter grabbed him.

"No, no," Walter said. "Don't wake your mother, Russ."

Eric squinted, confused and afraid. "When can I go home?"

"Go back to sleep and we'll talk about it in the morning. After breakfast. I'll make pancakes, how's that sound?"

"I'm not tired. When can I go home?"

"You're such a card, Russ." Walter laughed.

"Who's Russ?"

"Hey, I'm not tired if you're not. And I don't think the intruder is coming tonight, so you wanna play a game?"

"I want my parents. Can you call them again?"

"How about hide and seek?"

"What?"

"That was a good place you found earlier, behind the carousel. I almost didn't find you back there."

Eric started to cry.

"No, no." Walter put a hand over Eric's mouth and made calm shushing noises. "We gotta play now if we want to. Mom will be home soon and she always ruins the fun. C'mon, I'll show you."

* * *

It was a struggle, but Walter got Eric in the car. The boy was crying quietly as Walter buckled him in.

Walter ruffled his hair and said, "Be right back." Walter tightened his robe and walked to the side of the house to the trashcan.

The scrape of the plastic can dragging along the driveway woke Hailey up. She reached beside her for Walter and felt only blanket.

"Okay, so I was here, Russ, and you were doing like Oscar the Grouch does. You had been watching *Sesame Street* that morning. I remember. Before we played the game. That's where you got the idea. You and your impressions." Walter looked in the rearview. Over the horizon, he thought he saw the dawn peeking out, but it was the fires from downtown.

Walter buckled his safety belt and started the car. "Gin," he said. "I do remember that now. It was gin that day. I was drinking gin and knew I didn't have enough to get through the day." He drummed on the steering wheel as the memory came back. "And Hailey, your mom, was coming home soon. She wouldn't let me drive, that's smart of her. Never drink and drive, son. I mean that. So I had to make a run before she got back." Walter paused. He put his forehead on the steering wheel and continued, "It was her idea to bury you under the sycamore tree. She moved like a whirlwind, your mom. She had you in her arms, as I dug the hole under the tree. Like she'd been prepared for this."

* * *

Hailey had to wash the dirt off of Walter's hands for him. He was in a trance. The gin haze was wearing off and the reality of what had happened was gradually sinking in.

Before it could fully take hold, Hailey fed him the sleeping pills. It had been a steady diet of those ever since. But no booze. If Walter mixed them, he would die. Hailey drilled that into his brain. Like his very own version of the Alcoholics Anonymous serenity prayer—booze and pills will surely kill, with pills alone you will atone.

Hailey was certain the sleeping pills were a good substitute for alcohol. She was happy to see Walter shed the drinking weight and he didn't reek of bitter sweat all the time. There were some side effects –paranoia and hallucinations. But she figured those were more rooted in what happened to Russ than the pills them-selves. She had to be patient, she knew this. Be patient and she'd have her family back before summer. It was all she ever wanted.

* * *

She leaned inside Russ/Eric's room and flicked on the light. The sheets were all messed up. The comforter lay crumpled on the ground. "Walt?" Outside, she heard sirens coming over the hill.

"And I got in the car and I guess I just..." Walter choked up. "I just, forgot. I forgot we were playing the game. I had tunnel vision from the gin and I just, forgot." Sobbing now, "So I went to get booze. Like a coward. I wasn't thinking of you. I was selfish. And..."

The front door surged open and Hailey burst out onto the lawn. She made a screeching sound like a feral animal and ran with her arms outstretched towards her family.

"And I'm sorry." Walter said. "I'm nothing but sorry."

He threw the car in reverse and hit the gas. The car peeled out backwards down the driveway. Near the end, at the lip of the drive, Walter cut the wheel. The rear bumper missed the trashcan by a good foot and a half and hit the cop car dead on its side.

Walter put it in park and said, "You okay?"

Eric nodded. He was afraid, but somewhere in the back of his young mind he could tell that something important had happened. Without completely understanding why, Eric unbuckled his seatbelt, leaned over, and hugged Walter.

Walter smiled wide. "You little card."

He unbuckled and stepped out on to the street. The police officer was already out with his pistol trained on Walter. He was barking orders, but Walter couldn't hear him. The clarity he was feeling was louder than anything in the world.

Before the officer took him down to the pavement, Walter managed to call out, "See that! He's okay! Our boy's okay!"

SHARDS

1979

Peter has been getting up earlier and earlier, taking food from the kitchen and hiking down to Sunset Blvd. The streets are wide here and he can sit on the meridian and watch cars.

He can't understand why he doesn't have his own room. His aunt has her own room. His mother has her own room. Even the cleaning lady has her own room. But he has to sleep with his cousin. Peter's eleven. Skye is nine. Skye doesn't let him touch his stuff. Skye doesn't seem to sleep either, sitting up in his bed, scowling at the darkness.

He has two theories. The first one is that his mom had a roommate when she was in the rehabilitation center so maybe she thinks it's 'healthy'. The second one is based on something his aunt says, *"my house, my rules."*

The cars move pretty slowly in the morning and evening, so that's when he likes to be here. He can read the bumper-stickers better.

His favorite is the yellow one that says "I found it!" He scans the passing bumpers and when he spots one, he signs "I found it!" It took him a long time to figure out that "it" means Jesus. He thought "it" was a lot of things, but now he knows that "it" is Jesus. He has a bunch of questions he'd like to ask about this, but they'd be too difficult to sign. The only person who might be able to understand him would be Mrs. Babcock, his teacher. But she's back in Baltimore.

Nobody signs around here. He can't really tell anyone about the bad things that Skye does.

"Skye The Magnificent."

He misses their place in Baltimore. His mom wasn't home much, but he had a room and a TV and he could watch his VHS tapes whenever he wanted. His mom's boyfriend, Howard, was really into the Civil War. He gave him a super good VHS before he went away. It's narrated by Leonard Nimoy and has subtitles. It's about the start of the war at Fort Sumter in South Carolina.

A bunch of secessionists have surrounded the fort. Northern forces are trapped inside. All the Southerners want to be the first, to be the one to fire the first shot of the war. The tape stops here for a long time to talk about this. One historian says that Lieutenant Henry S. Farley did it, firing a 10-inch mortar round at the fort. Another says a guy named Edmund Ruffin did, shooting a 64 pound shell. Another guy says they all fired at once.

He imagines a bumper sticker that reads "I fired the first shot at Ft. Sumter!"

Skye scares him. He's been asking for a sword.

He imagines a whole load of bumper stickers. When his mom gets some money and they get out of here, he'll have them printed up and give them out as prizes.

"I aimed the cannon!" He'll give this one to the teacher who sent Skye to the principal. "I kept the powder dry!" For the neighbor who called the police about the tortured dog. "I lugged the cannon balls!" For the child safety official who got a court order to have a doctor look at him. "I lit the match!" For the psychiatrist who said they should send him away somewhere for help.

The problem is that none of this ever happened and Jacqueline came back from her Beijing trip with a Katana sword. When his mother acted concerned, Jacqueline reminded her that she was an alcoholic and that her son was deaf. They never spoke of the sword again.

"WHERE'S FARRELL?"
by Steve Newman

2015

HE WASN'T THE NICEST GUY SHE HAD EVER DATED. Or the smartest. Or the best looking. Sharyn was drawn to him because of a game they played, a sort of inside joke. They could be at a restaurant or at the movies, it could start anywhere. Gary would look around and say, "Where's Farrell?" Then she would look under the table or pretend to scan the theater. "I don't know. He was here a minute ago."

"You have no idea? You *are* his mother."

"I told you, 'Keep an eye on him.' I've been watching him all day."

They would glance around, each daring the other to crack. Finally, Gary would say, "Well, he couldn't have gone far. He's not walking yet, is he?"

"I hope not."

Ideally, there was someone nearby, preferably a parent, who would hear them and think god knows what. But they didn't need an audience. After a few weeks, they even played Where's Farrell? in bed.

"Not so loud," he would whisper, "you'll wake him."

"It's okay, I dropped him at your folks'."

"In Miami?"

She giggled, a point against her. "I mean I, *oh keep doing that.*"

"Where is he? Tell me or I'll stop."

"I left him in the Park. Just until we're finished."

Wherever they happened to be—her favorite was on the ski lift at Big Bear, that worried-looking man trapped between them— the game always ended the same way.

"Well, he couldn't have gone far. He's not walking yet, is he?"

"I hope not."

So when Sharyn discovered she was pregnant, the baby already had a name. They weren't planning a family, they weren't even married. A freelance proofreader for a small publisher, she had assumed she would delete "freelance" before becoming a real adult. But Where's Farrell? had developed a life of its own. The game made having a child seem doable.

"So where is the little bugger?" Gary asked, glancing at a menu. It was only a week since they had found out. "I mean how long are we supposed to wait?"

"Months, apparently."

The waitress brought a Scotch and a ginger ale. Gary took his and said, "Well, if he's late, we'll just dump him in the Park. No one keeps us waiting."

Sharyn knew this was for the waitress, still, she gave him a look. Kids picked up signals, she imagined, even in the womb.

They took a weekend in Vegas. When the minister asked if they had a witness, Sharyn said, "Yes, we brought a relative."

Gary ate it up. "Though he's a bit of a shut-in," he added.

Outside the chapel, the groom looked at the bride and shook his head.

"What's wrong?" she asked.

"The bastard. I knew he wouldn't show."

* * *

At three months, she felt a kick.

"Doubtful," said her doctor, sliding a stethoscope over her belly like a safecracker. "Probably gas. The fetus won't be mobile for another few weeks."

He was right, she felt no other kicks. Weeks passed. Where's Farrell? turned into Where's Farrell's Foot?

"Well, he's not a kick boxer," Gary said, "that's for sure."

He took her hand and brought it to his mouth. She expected a kiss but then he took her other hand and held it to his ear, turning her into an old-fashioned telephone. "Hello, Farrell? It's Daddy. Now, remember, you keep us waiting one day past—what is it, again?"

"September third," she said.

"—and we'll dump you right in the Park. You got it? Hello?" He dropped Sharyn's hands. "He hung up on me."

* * *

She knew before she was told. She took a picture of what was in the toilet and compared it to pictures online. So when the doctor made it official she just nodded. She had already "grieved," as the mommies online put it.

"I lost one before my first," the nurse said as Sharyn got dressed. "It's just nature's way."

"Of what?" *Making us miserable?*

"Getting it right, I suppose."

She couldn't tell anyone at first, even Gary. His job was operations, maximizing efficiencies. Aborting projects was the enemy.

I knew you couldn't keep your eye on him.

She decided to wait for the weekend to say anything, to give him time to process. Then Saturday came and he was in such a good mood, she put it off again.

"Hey, sunshine," he said, coming in from his run. "Why don't you get some air? You're moping for two, you know."

She took the car and drove, windows open. She wanted a breeze but the air just rushed out the back. She came to the Park which looked full of air. Perfect. *Brisk walks,* the obstetrician had prescribed.

The Park was empty. Just a jogger with a stroller he kept at arm's length, one of those Uberparents. There was also a stray in the bushes, following her. Either a dog ("Hi, Fella," she tried) or a large cat ("Hey, Missy"). The poor thing was too shy to show itself. On the path ahead, she saw a fuzzy green apple which turned out to be a tennis ball. She tossed it over the bushes. *"Fetch,"* she called, but the brush stayed still. Perhaps she scared the animal off. Or maybe it scampered back to its owner, not a stray at all.

* * *

The Park became her quiet place. By sunset it was often just Sharyn and Superdad flying by with his stroller. And the stray, the beast in the bushes, dogging her as she walked. It was a dog, she decided. It panted.

Gary remained in the dark. He was so playful and funny, she didn't want to spoil that. She knew he was more intense at work but what that looked like she couldn't say.

Then there were her parents and the lady at Rite Aid. How could she tell them before her own husband? Her proofreader's instincts kicked in. She couldn't erase the past but she could make corrections.

"Where's Farrell?"

"Now?" Gary asked, surprised to find her undoing his zipper. They were in the handicapped bathroom at the Getty. "I'm still numb from this morning. What's gotten into you?"

"Hormones," she panted, pulling down his boxers. "Being pregnant's an aphrodisiac, haven't you heard?"

He made sure the door was locked. "Guess it's nature's way of keeping me in the picture."

They rearranged their schedules to accommodate Sharyn's increased appetite. Before setting the alarm at night, they tried. As soon as it went off in the morning, they tried. Every day, around the clock, they tried. Well, she tried, he just got off. He wasn't sold yet on being a father, but being an *expectant* father, this was awesome. He owed Farrell big time.

* * *

It was mid-June, month six, when she actually saw him.

Gary said he'd be home late. "They're throwing me a shower at work. I'd invite you but you're not drinking, right?"

Which worked out. She had something to take care of. She had gotten her period a few days ago and needed to make a tampon run. Ordinarily, that just meant buying some but lately it was more complicated. She still hadn't updated Gary so her period required two tampon runs, one to buy them and one to throw them away. She kept the bloody ones in a knotted CVS bag which she disposed of in secret.

That evening, the Park was especially quiet. Superdad had taken the night off, but her other friend kept her company. She heard him scrabbling in the bushes nearby, or was that the CVS bag brushing against her? She held the bag more tightly and the sound stopped.

She came to a trash can and removed the lid. On top, glistening in the street light, was a discarded condom. She fumbled with the knot on her plastic bag, finally ripping it open. She dumped her used tampons on top of the condom. Something about a man's and a woman's fluids commingling in the garbage made her giggle. It was gross but since flushing Farrell, standing up to grossness felt necessary.

Then, crouching behind the trash can, there he was. Or she: fine-boned with shoulder-length hair.

"Hey, Missy."

Nothing.

"Hi, Fella."

Eyes.

Cloudy, snow-globe eyes. How old, five? six? Definitely a boy. His naked body was covered with scabs and fresh scratches. He avoided her gaze.

She reached into her coat for her phone but what came out was one of those protein bars she had been snacking on since January. She unwrapped it and held it out for the boy. He seemed interested but cautious, the way a dog might regard a new kind of biscuit. She tossed it on the dirt between them. He pounced on it, then disappeared in the bushes.

Driving home, Sharyn tried to make sense of what she had seen. Even before moving to L.A., whenever she saw something that defied reason, she thought, *They're probably just making a movie.* There was probably a whole cast of naked kids on the other side of the bushes, boys and girls in Dreamworks robes, sipping Perrier, texting. As soon as she got back to her computer, she would find out what dystopian thriller was shooting in Griffith Park.

Back home, as she got out of the car, she saw something else that defied reason. Barreling down the street, headed straight for her, was Superdad. The stroller led the way with Superdad giving it a shove every couple of paces. As he and Superbaby approached, Sharyn revised her assessment. For one thing, a woman's leg dangled over the side of the stroller. For another, Superdad was wearing Gary's favorite black boots.

"Are we home?" a voice asked from inside the stroller.

"Almost," said Gary. "We're at my place."

Sharyn shut the car door and started toward him. "Gary?" she called.

"Who's that?" the stroller voice said.

Believing there was no situation a peck on the cheek couldn't improve, Gary planted one on his wife's cheek.

"Look what the team gave me," he said, passing his hand over the stroller like a spokesmodel. "She's a beauty, right?"

Sharyn looked at the young woman reclining in the stroller. A blue high-heeled shoe made an uncomfortable-looking headrest. Sharyn was relieved that the girl at least had the rest of her clothes on.

"I'm Bethany," she said, and hiccupped.

From beneath the stroller, Gary produced an oversized greeting card.

"'*Happy Father's Day!*'" he read. "Isn't that sweet?" He opened the giant card and continued: "'*Here's hoping you're as good a Daddy to Farrell as you are to Operations! Love, Alicia, Megan, Glen, Bethany, Kevin, Heather.*' Isn't that something?" The names were scrawled in crayon, in different colors. '*Farrell*' was baby blue.

"Adorable," said Sharyn. "And you're just taking her for a little test drive?"

"Bethany needed some help getting home," he said quietly, and mimed taking a swig. "She lives just a few blocks away. I'll be back in two shakes."

"*One* shake!" Bethany yelled. "*Two straws!*"

"Oh, look," Sharyn said, closing the stroller's canopy, "it has a little awning."

Gary put an arm around his wife and pushed the stroller with his other hand. Sharyn figured they looked like the real deal, a family of three.

"You told them about Farrell?" she asked. "That's what you call him at work?"

"That's his name, isn't it? Don't tell me we're one of those couples that keep the kid's name a secret until it's hatched, like it's bad luck or something."

With that, he kicked the stroller into high gear and was off.

* * *

It turns out anyone can be pregnant if their clothes are loose enough. So even though it was July, Sharyn favored drapey sweaters, flouncy blouses, an old rain poncho (she stopped short of strapping a pillow to her belly). Gary never asked to see her changing shape. An operations guy, he didn't approve of nature taking its course. Bodies embarrassed him. Even before Farrell, he preferred Sharyn to wear something slinky to bed rather than nothing.

Where's Farrell? continued changing shape. It was August. He was in camp.

"Any letters from Farrell?"

"Nope. I guess he's busy."

"Busy jerking off. That's all I did in camp."

"He's not you, you know."

"Let's hope not."

Days were hot but the evenings were cool and the Park was perfect. Knowing the boy liked protein bars, she brought him many over the months. Also other goodies: blueberries, bananas, shredded carrots, even a Hershey bar (the online mommies would *not* approve). Once she brought him a half pint of milk and was up all night worrying—even she couldn't open those stupid milks. The next day she found the empty container on a tree stump. He had opened it like a pro. He always pretended not to see her. That was their game. But he saw everything. As soon as she put his food on the ground, wrapped in a paper towel to wipe his face, he would grab the snack and jump back in the bushes.

The First of September was cold and rainy. Sharyn's heart sank when it dipped below forty. But by the Third it was just overcast.

"How about a drive?" she said.

"Go for it."

"I mean both of us."

"Really? I just got home." He looked at the refrigerator.

"You can take it with you," she said. "I'll meet you outside."

Beer popping, he came out to the car just as Sharyn shut the trunk.

"Where we headed?" he asked. But as she turned the ignition, all she said was, "Seatbelts."

Although the sun was setting, the sky brightened as they drove.

"Look," he pointed, "the sun's final bow."

She squinted at the horizon. "You'll be a fun dad."

"Yeah, if the little prince ever makes an appearance. It's nearly Labor Day. Still no letters?"

"No. I mean *yes*. I didn't tell you? We got a postcard. It came today."

"No kidding, a postcard? That's it?"

They got off the Freeway and made the local twists and turns. As they slowed to a stop, the lights in the Park came on.

Gary said, "Ooh, creepy."

"No, it's not. It's beautiful."

"A little wild, if you ask me."

"Isn't it?"

Sharyn got out and went around to the back. "There's usually a few other people here. There's this dad and kid, they run together." She popped the trunk. "Actually, the dad runs"—she pressed a button on the stroller which snapped open—"the kid just sits there."

"I know who gets the better half of that deal."

"For now. Then it switches."

They started walking, pushing the stroller together.

"You mean this thing turns into a wheelchair?" he asked.

"If we're lucky."

They continued on the path, Sharyn on the inside, near the bushes. But it was Gary who first saw the boy. *"Look,"* he whispered.

A head poked out from behind the trash can. Sharyn put her hand on Gary's, signaling him to wait. She inched closer.

"Where's that good boy?" she said. Gently, almost singing: "Where's my good boy?"

More than just a head now. Scrawny neck, shoulders.

"There he is!"

He ducked back behind the trash can.

She gasped. "Where'd he go? Where's Farrell?"

The top of his head came out again, then his entire body. She took off her jacket but it was too rough and bulky. She removed her floppy flannel and held it open for him, a door that he stepped through. It fit loosely yet perfectly, like a robe. "That's better, isn't it? No more of those scratchy bushes, no sir. Nothing but the floppiest flannel from now on. You like that, don't you? Don't you?"

She pulled his hair out from under the collar. Gary put his beer in the stroller's drink compartment and stuck out his hand.

"Put it there, son."

The boy stared at the outstretched hand.

Casually, like it was the most natural thing in the world, Sharyn picked him up. He was tiny in her arms. When she placed him in the stroller ("Hello, Mr. Squirmy. You're not used to being held, are you?") there was room to spare. No chubby legs hung overboard.

Walking through the park, she and Gary took turns naming things they passed. The sights must have been familiar to the boy, but not their names.

"Bench."

"Tree."

"Squirrel."

"Moon."

Suddenly the moon was gone.

"Oh, no!" Gary said. "The moon disappeared! Is it gone for good? Where's the moon?"

Mouth open, Farrell looked at Sharyn. *Where'd it go?*

She rolled her eyes. "It's just a cloud, bear. The moon's still there. Daddy's only kidding."

Gary chucked his empty can. "We should get going. Least now we know where he is. Don't be a stranger, kid."

She lifted the boy out of the stroller and laid him on the ground. As she buttoned his floppy flannel, she whispered something in his ear.

Gary folded the stroller and Sharyn softly sang the boy to sleep. She left a protein bar in his shirt pocket.

On the drive home, she invented a new game.

"C'mon, I'm serious," Gary said. "What'd You Whisper To Him?"

Her part was easy. She just smiled and said nothing.

ECHO

2008

HE'D HAD DRY SPELLS BEFORE. But nothing like this.

Not a new Seeker in a month. Nothing. First, it was like there was no one around. Then, they were everywhere (pushing their strollers, nursing in the park, pushing the swings) but no interest, not a bit.

Marty'd even taken to doing follow-ups. Contacting people who'd feigned interest or lied that they had to run it by their spouse. These were, of course, a waste of time.

Today would be different! He'd hit all the parks from Atwater to Angeleno Heights. All the rec centers. The Mommy and Me classes. Baby Yoga. Sign ups for Soccer Basics in Eagle Rock were today, always promising.

Three hours later, he was driving aimlessly down Los Feliz Boulevard. It was a drought out there.

Even his Engagers, usually bubbly and irrepressible, were feeling it. They'd had great attendance at their Munch & Rap sessions—young moms at Silver Lake park, Hispanic nannies in Echo Park. The blankets they'd spread on the grass were filled, toddlers loved the crafts and sing-a-longs, but no one engaged. The hand-outs went untouched. Marty had even made an impromptu pitch. Nada.

He found himself parking at the Griffith Park Observatory. He'd been here once before, working an Explore The Stars/ Explore Yourself event. That was before the PWC had determined that night events weren't fruitful. Bed times, for one thing. Also, Sweepers like Marty tended to come off more menacing after dark.

Then it happened. If he'd learned anything over the last five years (and he should have by now), it was this: 'if it isn't impossible, it's easy.'

He'd barely crossed the lawn in front of the mighty stone building, barely had a chance to take in the sweeping view from Downtown to the ocean, had only just passed the tall obelisk dedicated to great astronomers of history, was approaching the bust of James Dean, when lightning struck.

"Excuse me, sir. Could you take our photo?"

"Why, of course. Here, with the view? Hold it! What a photogenic family. What a beautiful child. Walking yet?"

"Not yet."

"Ah, these are the best times. And also the most challenging, am I right?"

And he was off and running. He'd only gotten a few sentences into his pitch, about the joys and struggles of parenthood, hitting the "no reason to feel isolated because you're not alone," and had begun to tick off a few of the principles of the Parent Wellness Center when –

"That sounds great! When are these meetings?"

"We hold Coffee Chats at the Center at several convenient times, seven days a week…"

"How about right now?"

"Sure."

"Oh boyo! Let's go."

When he stood up to introduce them to the group, he knew he had a jewel. The crowd in the meeting room was all Mid to Upper level, a good number of Elevated-2s, several 3s, and even a few 4 and 5s. He could see it in their eyes as they took in the pair with the giant baby. This couple was irresistible. The indeterminate gender. The indeterminate sexuality. The unguessable race. And their *energy*.

So he kept if very short. "Brand new to the group." "Eager to learn. Eager to share." Here they are.

"I'll escort your young one to our Young People's Sharing Space and let you tell the group a little about yourselves."

The quiet one handed him the baby. It was much heavier that Marty'd expected. And the camera. "Don't lose that," she (he?) whispered harshly.

As the one named Tommy (Tommi?) stepped up to the microphone,

"This is great. I feel so welcomed. Oh boyo!"

Marty smiled his Closer's smile.

Tommy (Tommi?) spoke non-stop for the next thirty minutes. It was captivating. Her/his words came quickly, effortlessly. The language was full of imagery, the storytelling supported with vivid details, never slowing, always charging forward. And, above all, he/she was very involved in the tale, and enraptured with its telling.

Here is that story.

> The couple started the day with a celebration. A forgotten IRS refund check had been discovered under a pile of DVDs. It was like money from nowhere. Manna

from heaven. What a great start to a great day.

The celebration went on for hours until one of them said the word "baby." Now they can't remember how or why, and they had tried, believe it! Was it a word from a song like "Be My Baby" or "Baby Got Back"? Was it a slight admonishment for hogging the stuff? The origin was gone.

But that didn't matter. The important thing was that, right then and there, they began to think about the baby. Both of them. At the same time.

Next thing they knew, they were driving to Gramma's.

She was like "where have you been?" and "where is my money?" but all they could see was the baby. The baby was so big now! So beautiful. Their baby. Their own baby.

And they decided. Oh boyo. In a flash, they'd unlocked the crib and tucked the baby in the back of the car. Driving like crazy to get back to their place. Home.

Oh, the baby loved Home. But where would Baby sleep? Where would Baby sit? What would Baby eat?

They were sure doing a lot driving today. Oh boyo. Babies R Us. Ralphs. Target.

Back home, to assemble the high chair. Wash the new plates. The wonders of family life.

They need a family photo!

And driving again, straight to the observatory. They knew just the right stop. But, wait. No camera. Oh boyo.

Back in the car. The baby slid around in the back seat, slid all over the place. It was so funny. They bought the camera on Hollywood Boulevard. Even got a photo album.

Driving back, they played a fun game. Turning

pages in the album, imagining the photos and where they'd put them. Neither of them remembers where, but somehow "insert photo here" got be a running gag. Baby's first day at school—insert photo here. Baby's first car—insert photo here. Oh boyo. What a hoot.

The spot they wanted was right by the James Dean bust. They both loved that movie. Wouldn't that look great in the album?

Do you believe in miracles. Because I do now. Because the guy we asked to take our photo, the very first guy we saw, was Marty!

And so on.

From the Young People's Sharing Space, Marty could hear the talking but not the words. He'd been doing this for a long time. He didn't need to understand what was being said. He could read the room.

They were a big hit. Laughs broken by gasps turning into cheers. Solid gold!

The walls surrounding the small scattering of toddlers were decorated with the teachings of Pearl, the founder of PWC.

"Embrace the Unknown."

"Never Judge."

"There is No Room in this World for the Word 'No!'"

"However different *their* experience *seems,* the more like *yours* it *is!*"

The baby seemed to sense the positive reactions coming from the other room. Joe (Jo?) had been sitting since Marty had placed it among the other toddlers. Now, it seemed to waken, to stretch. It pushed against the floor with its chubby arms, wobbled to its feet on chubby legs.

"It's walking," shouted Marty, despite himself.

The baby teetered about the room. Seeing it among the other kids, Marty realized for the first time just how big it was. It was huge.

Marty readied the camera. What a moment!

Joe (Jo?) stopped next to a small child concentrating on a pile of blocks. Awkwardly, but with steady intent, the huge baby's hands went around the neck of the smaller one and closed. And squeezed.

The crowd cheered next door.

Marty was slow to act. By the time he reached the baby, it had lifted the gasping child off the ground by the neck. Marty pulled and coaxed but the baby was surprisingly strong. He finally got the baby to loosen its grip, but not let go. That would have to do.

Marty stepped back, winded. From this distance, it almost looked like the baby was hugging the child, comforting a crying playmate.

Another "oh boyo!" from Tommi (Tommy?) and an echoing response from the crowd. "Oh boyo!"

Marty snapped the photo. He just knew it would look great in next month's newsletter.

RAILS
by David Carpenter
1965

T WICE A YEAR, SOMETIMES EVERY FEW MONTHS, A CAR WOULD SLIP OUT OF PARK AND ROLL DOWN THE HILL. Miriam watched them from her bedroom window. She lived on Berendo Street and she was eight years old. Her bedroom was tucked by itself in a half-basement carved out of the slope. The cars were large and painted dull shades of tan or green, anticipating corrosion by the brown-spiced air. That morning, Miriam had watched a newish Buick Riviera glide past, drifting freely along the pavement then skipping along the raised curb like an overgrown puppy before rolling onto Los Feliz. She braced herself for the crash, the sharp moment when the runaway would surprise another car caught in its own reverie of speed. The quiet lingered then gave way to the disappointment, a dull bump. A bus bench maybe, or a weathered light pole.

Miriam knew that dinner conversation that night would make real what she had seen. Her teenage sister Sharon would detail the whole sequence with buoyant, heartsick enthusiasm. "That terrible, terrible accident" she would call it, or even "a real tragedy," conjuring details and context only a witness or perpetrator could know. Once she mourned the blind and toothless cat that had been trapped inside the car, a cat which was entirely and rather obviously imagined, but no matter. Miriam's sister did not like their neighborhood, did not like the city, did not like much of anything, and rushed into any opportunity to make this known, even with the consequences. Miriam's sister acted as if she was not afraid of their father's belt. Maybe she believed it was the city's belt, and their father merely the hill it sometimes rolled down. Miriam looked forward to hearing her sister's account this time, wondering what she would do with the disappointment of the ending. Would she sketch in some distressing carnage? Or would she find deeper truth in its absence, twisting the anticlimax into a simmering accusation?

Her father would listen patiently for a while and then cut her off. "Jesus, Sharon. Just like your mother." And that would be that.

Miriam turned from her window just as her bedroom door opened and her father stepped in. He looked exhausted. "We're going to the park. You'll want a hat."

* * *

Miriam rode the small train in the park for two hours, stopping every second time around and then again only one other time, when the man who drove the thing got off and disappeared for two minutes then came back. Her father had left Miriam with a handful of tickets and a few quiet words to the driver, but the tickets had been gone for some time. When the sun dipped behind the ridge the man stopped asking for them.

Over the past several months Miriam had come to think of the train as a creature, large, strong and inexpressive. The engine stood half as tall as her sister, and could keep going all afternoon. It pulled a dozen cars, each long enough to hold two people. The engine coughed and hissed and the train went on and on and on, a metal eel on tracks, tracing a misshapen oval between thin bushes and past a few child-sized buildings and through a tunnel at one end of the park. As the afternoon deepened, Miriam kept herself busy counting the turns, and then the trees, and then the pieces of trash along the siding. Each time the train completed its journey two times around and back to the start a new group of people came and went, mostly grown-ups. Some of the grown-ups seemed excited, others apologetic. They mostly ignored her.

Eventually the train stopped with a tired sigh and then silence. The man got off the engine and made his way back to Miriam. Miriam was alone now, and the shadow of the train stretched taller than the man. She sat atop a car the size and shape of a piano bench. She did not meet his eye.

"Your father left you here."

It was not a question. It was a fact, and Miriam already knew it.

"Said your mother would pick you up."

Something else she knew.

"Your mother here?"

A question this time, but not one for Miriam to answer. Even if she had an answer. Her mother's whereabouts and motivations were something Miriam was used to not knowing. She assumed the knowledge would somehow harm her.

Miriam wondered if her mother ever noticed how the train cars kept rolling and rolling, and if she knew that eventually they stopped.

"Anyone else coming?"

Miriam felt herself getting angry. She still did not look at him. This man took the tickets, he drove the train, he let the happy and the sad people on and off, and he even seemed to know many of them by name. Shouldn't he know if someone else was coming?

"Got a name?"

* * *

The shack looked small from the front. It was part of the scenery, an old west storefront built to scale and stained grey by diesel exhaust. But inside the door the shack opened into a good-sized room, with plywood walls and a concrete floor and a couch and a stack of magazines. The cover of the magazine on top had a photograph of a train, but it was torn. The only word Miriam could see was "Climbing."

"Make yourself at home, little Sharon. We'll get this figured."

"You live here."

"Sometimes. Not all the time. Yeah."

"Anyone else live here?"

"Like people? No. What about you? Do you live far away?"

Miriam pointed south, where she imagined the nearest houses might be.

"My father is a policeman."

"Well," said the man. "You'll want to eat. And I'll want to make a call. Sit tight." And then he walked back out the front door.

Miriam waited a moment, then followed him out the door. Twilight was fading, allowing the white-streaked rush of the interstate to bloom from behind the oleanders. Miriam smelled exhaust and train oil and the dissipating heat of an August afternoon. Miriam liked how the heat made her skin feel, the way it wrapped around, the way it would not go away even when you slapped and kicked at it. She liked the way it bothered her sister, who complained through the summer and well into fall, as if the heat were some sort of conspiracy, or an insult. Miriam knew this was true. Miriam was part of the conspiracy. She was someone who could feel heat rising off the ground, see it caress the tattered skin of eucalyptus trees, and watch it frame the mountains to the north with its upturned palms.

But in this park, away from the day lit pavement of the street that ran in front of her house, in the growing darkness of the trees and brush that covered the hills just beyond the tracks, the heat had given way to something else. It was something Miriam did not know about. And then, for a moment, that something else took shape. Behind the building where earlier in the day she had seen people buying snacks and soft drinks. It was not the man, it was smaller, and it was backing away. In the gathering darkness it was barely a shadow, clear but dim and painted in deep tones that anticipated the coming night. It moved so softly that she half expected it to drift up into the trees. A boy maybe.

She stood in the doorway, straining to hold the sight and make it real enough to keep, thinking to herself *I'll know it's real when we talk about it at dinner.*

* * *

He had a key to the snack bar because that is where the refrigerator was and that is where he kept his beer. In the winter he could leave it in the shack, when the late afternoon shadows were cold. But in the summer he needed the refrigerator.

Reaching toward the locked door in the darkness he fumbled the key and it fell to the ground. Failing vision and a full day's worth of glare did not help as he patted the ground, searching, wondering to himself what a child must think. They are grown up already, in their own ways, untroubled by the details of life, the baggage of experience. Fearless, at least sometimes. Had he been like that?

Inside he flipped on a light. He opened the refrigerator and took out a six pack. An unplugged cord caught his eye. He plugged it in and a radio came to life.

"…the mayor's call for all parties to remain calm seems to have been roundly rejected by certain elements of the commun—…"

He turned the radio off and went back outside. The sound of footsteps hurrying away caught his ear, but not his attention, as he relocked the door.

Back at the shack he found the door open and the light off. He leaned through the door and turned the light on. A girl stood in the middle of the room. Not Miriam. Older, maybe 16, and trying to look a whole lot older.

"Where's my sister?"

* * *

Miriam scrambled up the hill in the darkness. A deer trail, little more than a thin line through the sage scrub, obscure in the darkness. She moved quickly, but paused every few steps. Becoming still. Listening.

In the distance, further up the hill, the sound of something else moving through the brush, hurrying away.

Miriam pressed on uphill, pushing branches away. She imagined she was a rusty green car, rolling backward up Berendo Street, defying the rules of gravity. A magic car, avoiding the curb and tracing graceful S-curves along the way.

The brush cleared as she topped the hill.

In the distance she heard the sound of drums and bells and the whoops of young adults who were probably on drugs and wearing bell bottom jeans. Then, closer, down below, another movement of leaves and brush.

Miriam hurried down the hill, no longer pausing. With each step, the motion ahead seemed to get closer, and sounded more and more human. Not just the sound of movement, but breathing. Panting. Quick, hurried breaths, in rhythm with the beating pulse in her ears.

The noise stopped suddenly as Miriam emerged out of the brush and back into the empty darkness of the park. She frowned, surprised to find herself back so close to the train tracks and so close to the man's shack.

She was also surprised to see her sister standing in front of her. Sharon's face looked angry and the sleeve of her t-shirt hung loosely, half torn from its seam. The two girls eyed each other with complete familiarity uncomplicated by fondness.

"Where were you?"

"I thought I heard something."

"Up there? Jesus…"

"Did you see anything?"

"What do you mean?"

"I don't know. Running away."

"Jesus…"

"It knew I was following. It had to."

Miriam paused, waiting for another of her sister's complaints to blossom. But Sharon only looked away.

"Why are you here?"

"Because. Dad's not home."

"Mom?"

"Can't leave work. She says the army is there. Surrounding her building."

This felt new, like a place neither of them had been before, even though they both knew this part of the park as well as their own yard. This spot, with its clear view to the west and the south.

"Come on. The radio says we need to go."

That's when Miriam noticed the warm glow of not one sunset

but two. Twin orange flowers lighting up the night sky, one hovering somewhere far out over the Pacific, and the second rising up in the south, much closer, and growing.

P-22

2012

THIS IMAGE:

A mountain lion standing atop a precipice, looking over the body of his downed foe, a younger male. He is triumphant, now the undisputed king.

He surveys the land before him—a long unblemished forest, a river in the distance. A lone tree by his side.

His mate leaves him there. The dead mountain lion was her brother. She leads her tiny brood of cubs out of his hunting survey, far, far away from his jealous moods.

Over time, her cubs grow and bear cubs of their own. All girls. Who grow and bear. Who grow and bear. For nearly a century it goes on like this, until the first male child is born.

And this image is borne inside him. The hill. The tree. The forest and the river below.

He carries it with him as he leaves his home near the ocean. He moves steadily towards it, through Malibu and over the pass into Topanga State Park.

Across eight lanes of screaming fast cars on the 405. And now, the cities. Scurrying through backyards, cutting across streets at night, sleeping in alleys or storm drains during the day.

Like a pillar of fire burning before his eyes, the image guides him across the 101 at Universal Studios. From there, it's just another 10 miles around the reservoir and he's completed his 50 mile journey.

Once in the park, he climbs. When the path ahead is rising, he moves on. If it descends, he turns another way.

On the third day, he stands by the tree. Below, he can trace the criss-crossing paths he had followed here. Beyond is the river.

As the image of his ancestor's view fades, replaced by the city circling the park, the river made of concrete, so too does the image of his mighty ancestor. But, before it vanishes completely, he sees something new.

A small naked human by his side.

One day, not long after, he was caught in a trap. Rangers attached a tracking collar around his neck and dubbed him P-22.

People are interested in this lone mountain lion that has made such a perilous trek, only to live alone in the isolated park, surrounded on all sides by freeways that no other mountain lion had ever crossed, and probably never would. Leaving P-22 to live alone in the park.

Except he isn't alone. He has the boy.

BILLY CLOVER
by Josh Lawson and Tim Kirk

1964

T HE BARTENDER LINES UP THREE SHOTS ON THE BAR. Billy lifts the first and slides its contents down his throat. The liquor sets off fireworks and his eyes drift towards the trophy mounted above his head. He stares at the gnarled antlers through a faintly pulsating red fog. Other trophies are hung unevenly on the wood paneled walls. A buck, a boar, a ridiculous trout.

Welcome to the Avalon Tavern, Sulphur City, 84 miles southeast of Oklahoma City. Site of Billy Clover's homecoming party of one.

"Hey Billy, what do you say?" The smiling man is a study in contrasts. Greasy hair and jailhouse tattoos. Short-sleeved plaid shirt and polyester dress pants.

"Dick Dacklyn. How's tricks? Or is it your night off?"

"Hilarious, Billy. I heard you got out. How long you get this time?"

"Lucky number 3." It was like that. 3 years out. 3 years in. Stretching back 17 years to the halcyon days of Riverside Rancho, when his hair was still jet black and his physique was lean and relaxed, not wiry and wired.

"I figured you'd be heading back to Hollywood to cut another record!"

"Yeah, I'm gonna cut me a record. But I'm doing it over at Country Lanes. Oscar's joint. Me and Hollywood is taking a breather."

The Boy decides to show him something. A head reaching desperately from rushing water. Big eyes staring.

Billy throws down shot number 2, chasing away the image. "You still in the pharmacy business, Dick?"

"Well, since you still seem to be in the music business, we may be able to work something out."

"Set me up with a couple dozen bennies."

"Fifty will cover that. You need any weed? Seconal?"

"Naw. I'm one of those cats that needs to be up. That's me. I'm on the freeway when it comes to this shit, Dick. No time to slow down once I get started."

"No time to slow down, huh? Even when the bugs start crawlin' out of your skin?"

"Sometimes it makes for a good song."

"What's that one by Porter Wagoner? Not the one about the accident, but the other one."

Billy sings, "*In a building tall with a stone wall around, there's a rubber room. When a man sees things and hears sounds that's not there, he's headed for the rubber room.*"

"That's the one. 'The Rubber Room.'"

"*Illusions in a twisted mind to save from self-destruction, hmm it's the rubber room. Where a man can run into the wall till his strength makes him fall and lie still, and wait for help in the rubber room.*"

"Guy sounds like he's got a few screws loose."

"The man can write one hell of a song."

"Didn't you play with Porter?"

"Sure I did. But that was on 'Satisfied Mind.' I wish I were in on the new stuff. 'Skid Row Joe' off the new album, now that's a twisted song."

"You seen that album cover, with him in the Nudie suit, face all covered with sweat? That face, man, like honest-to-god anguish!"

"You can't fake that. Let's see these English boys top it. The music is changing alright, but boys like Porter and me know where it's going."

"Going straight to the nut house, you ask me."

"Yeah, when you get good and miserable, sometimes your work will show it. Hell, people love hearing about other people's misery. It sells records."

Dick tosses down a baggy full of blue pills. "Keep popping these bop pills, Billy, and you'll have plenty to sing about."

A sign reading "Country Lane Studios" hangs outside of a shabby storefront on a once-bustling street in Sulphur City. Better days. The windows are covered with old playbills. Faces peer out from sun-bleached album covers; either freshly-shaven fellas wearing sweaters or freshly-shaven fellas in cowboy shirts.

"The caller called Casey at half past four, he kissed his wife at the station door, he mounted the cabin with the orders in his hand, and took his farewell trip to the promis'd land."

Billy pours sweat inside the studio. He shakes a handful of bennies like a maraca, speeding like a freight train and singing about one that's out of control.

"He looked at his water and his water was low, he looked at his watch and his watch was slow, he turned to his fireman and this is what he said, 'Boy, we're going to reach Frisco, but we'll all be dead."

Billy pulls the headphones off and stares through a pane of glass at a confused face hovering over the recording board. The heavy man hits an intercom switch.

"What's the problem, Billy?"

"I can't get into this one. I mean, when did the old number nine crash anyway? Back in 1900-and-something and guys have been singing about it ever since."

Oscar scratches the skin under his toupee. "I guess what you're saying is you don't really feel what you're singing."

"Yeah, exactly. Shit, I got a ton of original material. Enough to fill the whole album."

"I understand that, Billy, but we need standards. Something familiar along with the new songs. Besides, that's part of your gift."

"What do you mean?"

"You're a chameleon, Billy, when you want to be. You can hear a guy sing just once, then you can turn around and sing his entire catalogue note for note, just the way he'd do it. It's scary how you do that."

"But it ain't me. It ain't my stuff."

"Well, this new stuff of yours is pretty different. It's not like your other hits. Let's face it, it's no 'They Call That Gal My Mama' or 'He's Somebody's Hero' or even 'Cabin On The Hill.' Good, wholesome tunes. This new stuff…it's dark, man. It's really dark."

"That's where I'm feeling it, you dig? I gotta follow my muse."

"Well, you've been right before. And, hey, getting dark and edgy worked for Johnny Cash, Porter and the Louvin Brothers. Who knows, maybe it'll work for Billy."

"You gotta trust me. It's 1964, man. Things are changing. This is where the music is going."

Oscar sighed. "I believe in you, Billy. But you have to meet me half-way. You know what happens when you go too far."

Billy does. He nods, sobered. "I can make him understand."

"Him?"

"Forget it. Let's cut this thing! Let's shake a tail feather here, Oscar!"

Oscar counts him down. Four, three, two, one.

"I like your music, Billy. Have some potatoes."

Billy takes the plate from his mother. She's all dressed-up for dinner in her Sunday dress, even though they are eating in the kitchen. Billy passes the plate, untouched, along to his brother, Johnny, just home from work at the mill.

"I know you do, Mama. But I'm wasting my talents. That Oscar, with his oldies and his songs about God." Billy looks to the heavens. "No offense, Lord. I just don't feel people should be making money off your glory."

"Such a good boy."

"It's good to be back, Mama."

"Next time you're singing and playing on one of those TV shows, you should do some of your impressions. You should do Jimmy Hart."

"Mama, no one knows Jimmy Hart unless they grew up on this very block."

"But it's so good, Billy. You sound just like him, and you got his walk down too."

Johnny laughs. "What now, Billy? When you making your big comeback?"

"Comeback?! Where you think I've been?"

"In the State Penitentiary! You're a five-time loser. And I'm sure they never get you for the real bad stuff you've done."

"What's that, Johnny?" Mama's hearing aid lies unused next to her plate. It makes her ears itchy.

"He's just yapping. You know Johnny." Billy leans close to Johnny and lowers his voice. "You're right, I've done far worse things than anything they ever put me in jail for. It's all been drink and drugs to them."

"Glad to hear you're completely rehabilitated!"

"Mama don't know nothing about me. She don't want to hear about the women and my bad ways. Play her game, make her happy, and just let her keep thinking she has something to be proud of in me. You know as well as I do, I'll never change."

"What are you saying, son? I can't hear you boys."

"You keep up the way you are, Billy, and you'll break her heart for good soon enough. How you think she'll take it if her oldest boy is found face down in the parking lot of the Avalon Tavern?"

"Beats the shitter. That thing's filthy."

"Keep cracking jokes, Billy. The last joke will be your funeral. The only people there will be me and her."

"What are you boys talking about?"

"Nothing, Mama. I'm just asking Johnny to step out to the bar with me. Like lovin' brothers do."

"I'm not going, Mama. I got to sleep."

"You're a lucky man, Johnny. You can sleep at night. Not me. There's a boy that lives in here." Billy raps his head with his knuckles. "He's dirty and hairy and he don't know one word from another. But he knows me. He's seen what I can do."

"Maybe you should get some professional help, Billy."

"I do." Billy tilts an imagined bottle. "Every night."

Oscar plays a freshly cut single in his office. If your prized possessions are a gold record album and a couple of gold-plated bowling trophies, then yellow would be among the worst colors to paint your office walls. Oscar's office is yellow.

Billy pounds a beat on his desk, singing along.

"*The current tore you from my grasp, you sank into the deep, I will swim the mighty river, and dive until my breath gives out, and there, my love, we will find our forever sleep.*

His face popping sweat, he looks expectantly at Oscar.

"Personally, Billy, I don't get it. I can understand one or two songs about a dead broad. But six? I can't sell that. Maybe at the loony bin, but not in the record store."

"What the hell do you expect from me? A record full of worn out standards? I told you, that ain't me!"

"Shit Billy, I'd be happy with something halfway sane. I mean, you decide to do a cover and it's "Psycho". Don't get me wrong, I like the novelty of the "Psycho" single. We might be able to sell that. But then you got the Peeping Tom song, which is pretty fucking creepy. And it just keeps going and going. You're singing about killing, about shooting up hard drugs, boozing, and now this one, it sounds like necrophilia!"

"This track is about a long-lost love and a guy going all out to be with her. Ever hear of a little ditty called 'Romeo and Juliet'? That one was written by William Shakespeare, mister!"

"When you said you had some stuff going on in that head of yours, I had no idea."

"You know what, Oscar? You wouldn't have any idea. There

ain't too many of us out there that think this way. I wouldn't expect you to see the whole picture."

Billy is on his feet. "We shall now part ways. It's been nice working with you, Oscar, and I'm sorry it has come to this. I really am."

Oscar laughs. "Billy, are you serious?"

"Afraid so." He scoops up a stack of singles. "I'll consider this payment in full."

"Clover, you are one nutty fellow. You ever thought about maybe checking into one of those sanitariums? It might do you some good. When you clean up your act, come back here and we'll work something out."

"Oh yeah? Look at Van Gogh. They all thought he was crazy. See you on your way down, Oscar."

The receptionist is listening in the hallway, and Billy nearly knocks her over as he careens towards the door. He pauses to scatter some papers and records across the room. He rips the wooden "open" sign from the window and throws it out the door ahead of him.

The room feels very empty after he's gone.

"May I say something, Mr. Lane?"

"Go ahead, Martha."

"That man scares me."

"You and me both."

The drinks are going down quickly. They are just disappearing from Billy's hands. Everything is too bright. Too clear.

Waylon Jennings is on the jukebox. His voice has a sharp crack in it, like cold winter air. He sings about how something is wrong in California.

Dick in his polyester suit sidles up next to him. "Barkeep, gin and tonic for my friend. A Chivas for moi. And whatever old Billy here is spilling on those native duds of his."

"Dick, you son of a bitch. I've been looking all over for you."

"Billy baby. You know Spike, don't you?"

Billy stares at the skinny hustler. It's so bright inside his head that he sees every detail, every feature in sharp relief. The leather pants and tight shirt, the bright red hair. The fake mole on his upper lip. The line of stitches above his pencil-thin eyebrows.

"Shit, man, did I do that to you?"

The lovers laugh.

"You idiot, Clover. That was from his last trick."

"Hey, watch your fucking mouth, Dick! I don't even know the guy!"

"That never stopped you."

They grope and giggle. Dick's tongue looms large. Spike's lips pucker and expand, beckoning red and wet.

Billy's hands shake, spilling his drink all over the place. He gives up and tosses it behind the bar. "Hey, Dick. You got what I need?"

Dick slides out a bag full of pills, blue and black and red. "What you got me for me?

Billy pulls the stack of 45s from his coat. "These are singles of my latest. Fresh off the presses. Probably worth a lot. Look. I even signed them."

"I can't give you much for those."

"Check it out! The b-side is 'Psycho'. Blind Leon Payne wrote this fucker. Eddie Novak had a hit with it." Billy begins to sing.

I saw my ex again last night, Mama

She was at the dance at Millers store
She was with that Jacky White, Mama
I killed them both and they're buried
Under Jacob's sycamore
You think I'm psycho don't you, Mama?
Mama pour me a cup
You think I'm psycho don't you, Mama?
You better let 'em lock me up."

Dick and Spike exchange a look. Dick shakes his head.

"Well, how about this, then?!" Billy points a revolver at Dick's forehead. His hands are shaking bad.

Spike gasps but Dick just laughs. He empties the bag on the bar. "Take what you need and get out of here, you fucking nut."

Billy scoops the entire pile into this mouth and runs.

Scrub brush fills every empty space in this part of Sulphur City, every unplanted yard, every forgotten meridian or street divider. So when the brush ends and the gravestones begin, you know right where you are. Where all roads end.

Billy weaves between the headstones, stumbling on the markers. He pulls an artificial flower from a cheap vase. He sticks it in his lapel. Which cracks him up. He whistles, which cracks him up some more.

He stands over his father's grave.

RYAN "PAPA" CLOVER.

White lights flash in Billy's eyes. He looks around for head-lights, but it's all in his head.

"Here you are, you old bastard, and here you stay! You never got nowhere. Not like me! I sold out the Riverside Rancho every time I played. I played with Jimmy Wakely, Spade, Tex Williams, Lyle Talbot, the Texas Playboys, all the greats! When I heard you croaked, I was playing the Palomino. The Palomino, you fuck! I raised a bottle for you that night and told the whole audience, 'My Daddy's dead. He never did a kind thing in his life. All he ever wanted was one thing - to get the hell out of Sulphur City. But he never did.' And here you are! You're still here!"

Billy hacks and spits at the headstone, but it only ends up on his shirt. He wants to piss on the grave, but that isn't going to happen either.

He hears something. A rustling somewhere nearby. Something scurries past in the shadows.

"Is that you?" Billy spins an awkward 360. "You out there?" His eyes wildly search the darkness. "I thought you couldn't leave them woods in California. I thought I'd outrun you."

Billy sounds scared. He tries to regain some bravado by lighting a smoke. Cigarettes scatter over his boots. "The Bug-Bear—far from home! Couldn't get enough of Billy's thing, huh? Billy doing what Billy does."

The Boy shows him Maddie, bloody and crying in the moonlight. Billy drags her out of the woods. Ahead is a tunnel. It leads under the freeway.

"Were you watching when I dumped her in the river? Were you laughing when she screamed all the way down the river to the sea? I know I was. I know Billy was laughing up a storm!"

Frantically waving arms. Cresting the water, disappearing from sight.

Billy's laugh turns into a choking sound and then a weak gasp. He slides down the gravestone. His eyes are searching but they aren't finding anything. The sound in his ears sound like the river.

"You and your fucking picture show." The lights are going out, one by one. "At least you came to see me go."

Of course, Johnny was right. It was only him and Mama at the funeral. The preacher left early. They buried him right next to his father's grave.

LAST HIKE TO BEE ROCK
by Tim Davis

2018

GUS PARKED THE CAR IN A FAR CORNER OF THE GRIFFITH PARK GOLF COURSE PARKING LOT. The sprawling lot serviced two 18 hole courses, Wilson and Harding, named after our 28th and 29th presidents respectively. As he turned off the car, Gus imagined for a moment Woodrow Wilson in the Great Beyond wondering how the hell he wound up being paired for all eternity with that fool Harding. Were the Park committee members so lazy, were their imaginations so restricted that they only allowed themselves to choose successive presidents for the two course names? And if there was some convention that only permitted sequential naming (for Godsakes, who comes up with such conventions?!), couldn't they at least have put me next to my predecessor? Taft, Gus imagined Wilson imagining, would have made a much worthier next door neighbor.

Taft, Wilson, Harding. Regardless of their party affiliations, whether you agreed with their politics, whatever you thought of their performances in office, there was no denying each had lived a life of consequence.

That's how Gus was thinking about them anyway—consequential men, all—at this juncture. This particular juncture being the one that had led Gus Hayward on this particular mission on this particular Tuesday afternoon.

My beautiful boy,

I don't expect you to understand what I've done. (I guess I should say what I'm doing... *but* what I will have done *by the time you read this.) Honestly, I hope you never do. I hope you never face the same reckoning I have, nor know the same anguish. Nor arrive at the same solution for extinguishing your pain.*

More than anything, my greatest hope for you is that you won't wind up like your old man.

Gus crossed Griffith Park drive, the steep, Valley-facing hillside looming. Unconsciously, he pressed his key fob to lock the car door behind him. He'd walked only a few steps further before a conscious thought brought him to a complete stop. He held up the key again and pressed the unlock button twice, now leaving all his car doors unlocked. What did he have to protect at this point anyway?

Gus took a big sip of water as he passed the first sign to Bee Rock. He noticed a threesome strolling leisurely down the fairway on Harding's first hole, which ran parallel to the first part of the trail. He remembered first learning to play in his 20's on the 9-hole Roosevelt course, a few miles west from here just down Vermont Avenue from the Greek Theater. Gus never cared much for the game, but he loved playing Roosevelt on the afternoons before a big concert.

Listening to Billy Joel fuck up the lyrics to *Piano Man* during a soundcheck while surveying a 10- foot putt for par was a distinct Griffith Park-ian pleasure.

Such pleasures were echoes of faint echoes to Gus now.

His thoughts were unspooling thusly as he trudged along the poorly marked trail towards Bee Rock. The rock was aptly named (he almost audibly scoffed to himself); the site of the cruelest sting of his childhood. Clambering up the trail, Gus's mind showed no signs of relaxing its relentless swirl.

I've made plenty mistakes in my life, but you my boy were not one of them. You were the best thing I ever did, the only thing I can look upon with any sense of accomplishment. The only thing I did that mattered. The only mark I'll leave on this world.

If you greet the news of my exit with anger, shame, or disgust, no one will blame you. My prayer is that in addition to whatever other feelings may arise, you'll also experience some measure of the relief that I've felt since I made this decision.

To say Gus Hayward had lived an inconsequential life, or one that had at least NOT turned out as planned, would be an understatement. It would also be inaccurate. Gus had never managed to put together much of a plan about anything further out than two weeks ahead. And it's a pretty safe bet that had he managed somehow to cobble together a plan for the future… say, for the mid-life in which he currently found himself enmeshed… he certainly wouldn't have planned for *this*.

"This", aka a snapshot of Gus's life:

- A once promising career writing scripts for commercials (remember the one about the 2 brothers taking a road trip through the decades in a procession of Toyotas? That was Gus.), reduced by various addictions and misguided life choices to a series of odd jobs that left him scrambling to make his nut every month;

- A "nut" that included child support to his ex-wife, Nina; his portion of a private school tuition for their teenaged son, Jackson; a staggering IRS debt, and payment plans to a variety of creditors courtesy of the above-mentioned poor life choices;

- A personal life, such as it was, that consisted of binge-watching old tv shows, the occasional Tinder date, and thrice-weekly, ever less joyful "self-soothing" sessions. Gus remembered the term being used once by a therapist of his, and he seized upon it as it seemed slightly less pathetic to him than "choking the chicken", "bashing the bishop" or "polishing the family jewels".

- A tortured mind relentless in the volume and mass of critical judgements it generated, each one aimed at the vessel which contained it. These judgements always pierced more deeply on special occasions, such as the anniversary Gus was "celebrating" that day.

All of it... *this*... leading up to one final hike. Gus's hike of atonement.

My pain came partially at least from some of the same sources which plague us all. Heartbreak, loneliness, and despair have been companions for as long as I can remember. It kills me... literally... that I wasn't able to save my marriage with your mother. As hard as it may be for you to imagine, she and I once loved each other with all our hearts. Which is another way of saying that you came from love, even if you didn't grow up seeing or feeling as much of it as you deserved.

But you also sprung from a deep well of pain. Your mother's as you know was not of her own doing. Her pain arose largely as a result of the neglect and abuse she suffered at the hands of her own family. I always admired how she broke free of those bonds and became the loving, kind and patient mother she did, even though she had none of those qualities modeled for her as a child.

The brightest spots in Gus's life came on the occasions of seeing his boy, Jackson. But those had been dwindling ever since Nina had remarried a prosperous cardiologist (really, who'd ever heard of a down-on-his-luck cardiologist) who was able, finally, to provide Jackson with a level of comfort and stability he'd never experienced with Gus. Gus felt the boy, only 15, had already grown tired of the few activities Gus managed to arrange for them.

Hiking in Griffith Park, in fact, was one of the few remaining father/son outings Jackson still seemed to enjoy participating in. Jackson's favorite was the one that started off at the Griffith Park Visitor Center, wound up a gravel fire road before opening up onto a wide single track that climbed and dropped down several steep ridges. The trail finally lead to an asphalt road from which they would emerge at the very top of Griffith Park, right above the Hollywood sign. Each time they reached this perch, father and son would grab each other's hands and raise them triumphantly, like a winning relay team, and call out at the top of their lungs, "We're the kings of Hollywood!"

It was a hokey gesture, inspired by a hokey movie, but it was a tradition they'd clung to for years. Those moments formed a collective memory Gus hoped he'd be able to take with him where he was headed next.

Gus had never had the heart to take Jackson up to Bee Rock. Nor would he ever.

As for my own suffering, I can find no one else to blame but myself. Believe me, I've tried. I used to accuse your mother of forcing me to pay for the sins of her father. Uncle Jeremy was an asshole for ignoring me for the entire duration of our childhood; Poppa Jack for setting such high standards of excellence. I even resented your grandmother for loving me unconditionally. Maybe if I'd had to work a little harder for my own mother's love, I wouldn't have been so disappointed when the rest of the world failed to embrace me as eagerly as she did.

I nursed all of these resentments for years before I finally realized I was only causing myself greater pain.

After a stretch on a fire road followed by several wrong turns—wrong turns were as plentiful on the hike to Bee Rock as they had been in Gus's life—Gus finally found himself on the right trail. Narrow at points with tiny branches nipping at his calves like an annoying pup, Gus was nonetheless able to look up ahead and confirm that this last part of the trail, cutting through the thick brush that covered the hillside, was in fact leading him to his final destination.

His destination and the focal point of distress from which he'd been running for over 40 years.

Thank God those resentments eventually faded... or healed... or maybe a little of both. Or maybe I just grew tired of playing the victim. The bummer is, as I released each of those resentments one by one, I found them being replaced by an even greater resentment towards someone I am apparently unable or unwilling to forgive.

Gus was a man not so much haunted by his past, as consumed by it. He often felt as if he were driving a car whose rear-view mirror and front windshield had been swapped. Where most people saw their present directly in front of them and their future on the horizon of life's highway, Gus looked out the front window and saw his past spread out wide in front of him. It was a past present for him in every waking moment. His present and future, on the other hand, were reduced to a mere sliver in Gus's field of vision.

Gus peered through the sliver and saw the familiar pockmarks of Bee Rock just around the bend. Cresting the ridge, he was surprised to see fencing surrounding the uppermost part of the rock. As he drew closer still, he could tell from the rust and wear and tear on the fence that it had been in place for a long time. Too bad it hadn't been there when he and Jimmy first made the climb back in 1974. 43 years ago to the day.

But who was counting?

> *You still have the best of me within you. The boundless curiosity, sense of adventure, and love of music are my legacy, boy, and it's awesome to see how thoroughly you've made them all your own. I just hope I'm taking the worst with me—the decaying, poorly cared for body; the overly critical mind rendering negative judgements of everyone and everything in its path; the financial anxieties which I served up to you in larger portions than any teenager should reasonably be expected to consume; the dormant, easily triggered melancholy.*

Jimmy Margolis had been the star of no less than 50 of Gus's bedtime stories when Jackson was a kid. Jimmy and Gus were morphed into the thinly veiled characters of "Timmy" and "Russ", two heroic kids who could be counted on to get into and out of a variety of sticky situations in 6 or 7 minutes, roughly the amount of time it took for Jackson to drift off to sleep. It made sense that Jimmy was the star of these stories, since he'd pretty much been the star of Gus's entire childhood. At least up until the age of 11, when he became the victim of it.

Gus, of course, had told Jackson what happened to Jimmy. How could he not? It was part of Gus's primordial ooze. But *what happened to Jimmy* had never been fashioned into a bedtime story, or any story for that matter. The material was still too raw and close to the bone for Gus to hold at enough of a distance. No matter how much time had passed, no matter how much therapy he attended, no matter how many substances he consumed, Gus had never managed to gain the perspective necessary to tell the story.

God knows he'd tried. He'd replayed that day in his mind probably a million times over the years, sometimes willfully reaching for it, other times accepting its appearance like an old familiar movie you come across while channel surfing in the middle of the night. Each time he found himself unable to change the channel; each time he hoped it would end differently. And even though he knew it wouldn't... you can't change the past, after all, you can only run from it with a grim mix of panic, horror, and desperation... even though the end never came as a surprise, the pain of the loss cut Gus just as sharply every time the memory surfaced from the ooze.

EXT. BEE ROCK TRAIL—DAY (1974)

Two 11-year-old boys (GUS and JIMMY), pals since birth, scamper up the trail and onto this rock outcropping looking north over the Valley.

JIMMY
Holy shit, what a view!

Jimmy steps out further onto the rock, peers down over the edge.

JIMMY
Come here, man. You gotta check this out.

Gus stays several large paces behind his friend.

GUS
That's okay. I can see it just fine from right here.

JIMMY
Don't be a pussy.

GUS

I'm not a pussy. I'm just scared of heights is all.

JIMMY

Gus buddy, that is the definition of pussy.
Come on, I promise, you'll be safe.

Reluctantly, Gus takes a few steps closer to the precipice. As he slowly draws even with Jimmy:

GUS

I'm not a pussy.

JIMMY

I didn't say you were. I just said don't be one.

Gus soaks in the view. Clearly exhilarated. He hollers. A loud ECHO bounces back from the valley below.

JIMMY

See? What'd I say? Cool, right?

GUS

Waaaaa-HOOOOOO!!!!

Gus's "HOOOOO" rings out in the distance. The boys crack up. They hear a WOMAN'S VOICE from far below on the trail:

OMAN'S VOICE (O.S.)

Boys? Everything ok?

JIMMY

(yelling back) Yeah, mom. We're fine!

Gus picks up a rock and points into the distance.

GUS
Check this out.

In one graceful motion, Gus gives the rock a mighty hurl. It arcs out and over a thin hiking trail snaking up the mountainside.

JIMMY
Damn. You got an arm on you!

GUS
Yeah, I do. Bet you can't throw it that far.

JIMMY
Probably not. You're the pitcher.

Jimmy bends down and picks up a golf ball-sized rock.

JIMMY
But fuck if I won't try.

Tossing the rock lightly in his hand, Jimmy steps out further onto the rock looking for a good launch point. From where Gus stands several steps behind, it looks like his friend is at the edge of the rock.

GUS
Hey. That's too far. You gotta throw it from back here.

JIMMY
Says who?

A man's voice answers from behind:

MAN'S VOICE
Says me.

Gus looks up and sees a MIDDLE-AGED MAN looking

down at him. It's OLD GUS from the future.

> YOUNG GUS
> Who are you?

> OLD GUS
> Your friend is way too close to the edge. You can see that, right?

Standing at the edge of the rock, Jimmy begins to windmill his arm in preparation to throw. He either can't hear the two Gusses, or he's ignoring them.

> YOUNG GUS
> So what am I supposed to do?

> OLD GUS
> Stop him.

> YOUNG GUS
> He's Jimmy. I can't stop him. No one can.

> OLD GUS
> Genius idea challenging him to a throwing
> competition from way up here.

Young Gus looks up at his older self and scowls.

> YOUNG GUS
> You're a fucking asshole.

> OLD GUS
> You got that right.

> YOUNG GUS
> *Who are you?*

Out on the rock Jimmy finishes his windup and heaves the

rock with all his might. His throwing motion has none of Gus's grace, but what Jimmy lacks in athleticism, he more than makes up for in gusto.

His plant foot comes down hard on a loose rock, which quickly gives way under his weight.

YOUNG GUS/OLD GUS
JIMMY!!

As Jimmy slips off the edge, young Gus falls to his knees in horror.

THE GUSSES' P.O.V.—An empty space on the rock where Jimmy stood just a moment ago. Before he fell into the abyss. Before he became inextricably woven into Gus's history and future, haunting each present moment as it approached and ticked past.

Young Gus is no longer aware of old Gus, even when he (old Gus) places a comforting hand on his (young Gus's) shoulder.

OLD GUS
I'm sorry.

Jimmy's mom, a vision of 70's loveliness in halter top and a cowboy hat, emerges from the trail and steps up onto the rock. She immediately senses something wrong.

JIMMY'S MOM
Gus? Where's Jimmy?

Old Gus couldn't face her then, and he can't face her now. He leaves young Gus beginning quietly to sob on his knees, and slowly makes his way out to the edge of the rock. Behind him panic settles over Jimmy's mother; dread and despair over young Gus.

As old Gus peers over the edge, we...

DISSOLVE TO:

EXT. BEE ROCK - PRESENT DAY

Gus stands closer now to the edge, time in transition. Behind him, young kneeling Gus SLOWLY DISAPPEARS... as the fence SLOWLY FADES INTO PLACE.

There's a hole in the fence, large enough to allow a grown man to slip through.

> *Since I cannot forgive myself for all my various short-comings and inadequacies, I won't ask you too, either. All I will ask is that you remember how much I loved you and how much joy you brought me since the moment you entered our lives.*

Gus takes one last look out from Bee Rock. The view hasn't changed much in the last 40 years. In the distance, out past the LA River and the 5 Freeway, lies the industrial section of Glendale. Tracking in from the horizon, Gus sees the back nine holes of the Wilson course. Still closer, he can make out the same hiking trail towards which he'd launched the rock decades ago.

He steps out onto the very edge of the rock. There are no steps remaining but down. Gus's past, present, and future have all telescoped into this one moment. Time past and time future, each pointing inward towards this inevitable end.

> *Even this, Jackson, this hideous act of cowardice, this betrayal of your faith in me, is offered up as an act of love. I don't want you to see me like this anymore, nor be forced to endure my pain as your own. The most loving gift I can give you at this point is your freedom from me.*

"Hey. That's too far."

Perched now at the precipice, Gus swivels his head around, half expecting to find his younger self there issuing a futile plea for sanity, restraint, and self-preservation. Instead, Gus sees a half-naked boy with a tangled mop of dark hair hanging over black eyes.

The boy says nothing. He simply cocks his head and looks curiously at Gus. Has he come to save Gus, or is he daring him to jump? Or does he perhaps not give a shit about Gus at all?

The boy takes a step forward. Gus experiences a jolt of fear. *Holy shit. This kid's gonna kill me.* The fear subsides as the boy, his expression unchanged, slowly extends his hand. A moment passes. The boy waits for Gus to reach back.

> *Hah. He doesn't want to kill me… he wants to save me.*

Gus suppresses a laugh. He had taken enough screenwriting classes to know a Deus Ex Machina when it was staring him in the face. And he wasn't biting. Not today anyway.

Gus turns away from the boy, undeterred. He gazes once again at the view. The drop. His destiny. He takes one last deep breath, filling now with an even greater sense of peace and resolve.

> *So enjoy it, Jackson. Enjoy your freedom. Enjoy your life. And imagine me looking on with a smile. Because I will be.*

> *Eternally yours,*

> *Dad*

At last, there were no more thoughts. No more words. No more pain.

Gus Hayward was done.

SHARDS

2019

CHRISTY CAN WALK TO SCHOOL, BUT SHE HAS TO TAKE THE BUS TO GRIFFITH PARK. Every morning, she attends her classes and then her extra-curricular activities. She's on many clubs and teams which require her to stay late at school. At least this is what her parents believe.

She does her math homework on the bus after school and composes her writing assignments in her head during the long hike into the hills, printing them carefully in her notebook as she sits in the brush and waits. The last bus back to the valley leaves at 2:50 am. She's always on it, catching a little sleep here and then a little more after she slips in the back door of her parents' house. She's up before the rest the family so that she can shower away the dirt and muck and clean the tub.

If this schedule is wearing her out, she doesn't show it and her parents and teachers have no other reason to suspect she has a secret life. Her grades are top-notch, she excels on the swim team and in karate competitions. She's captain of the drill team and holds a position in student government. She took Freddy Green to the Sadie Hawkins dance and he took her and some friends to Sea World for his birthday. She attends all of her brother's soccer games and helped her little sister to mend her ballerina outfit after it got caught on an old nail in the garage.

The shadows are long as she reaches the entrance to the fire road. She checks the lock on the gate. This moment decides the rest of the evening. If it's locked, then no vehicle can get past and there's no reason for her to be here. *They* need a car or truck to transport a body. If it's locked, then she'll turn around and head home.

But this has only happened seven times in the two years she's been coming around. The rangers seem to have forgotten what happened here.

She shivers a bit in her purple and black uniform with the Valley Vista logo. She slips on a sweatshirt and pulls the hood over her long hair.

At first, she used to follow the road as it crisscrossed its way to the spot. Then she discovered a short-cut. The path is steep and her calves burn.

She rejoins the road as the sun is setting. She picks up her pace, making sure to find the craggy rock that marks the spot. The grove of California oak is straight ahead. She settles in their midst and she waits.

The news reports had featured extensive footage of the scene— correspondents reporting near the distinctive rock or this grove of oak. That made it possible, made it possible to find. There were even remnants of dried blood on these leaves the first time she found it.

Over the years since she started coming here, she has read in the papers of bodies found in other remote areas of the South-land. But never here. They haven't been back. Not since that night.

Faith.

The moon rises. Christy pulls her uncle's journal from her backpack. She likes to read it out here.

When she was eleven months old, her father fell and shattered his body. Her mother began working double shifts and her father was in the hospital for a long time, so her uncle Mickey came up with a plan. He changed his hours at the warehouse to the midnight shift. That way, he could pick up Christy every morning and get her out of the house and into the world. At night, he'd drop her with a sitter, jotting down some notes in a journal, describing for her parents what their daughter had done that day—a trip to the playground, to the zoo, to look at trains, or to ride the carousel that sits silently in the dark valley somewhere below her. Sometimes these notations were just a few lines, hurriedly scribbled as he rushed off to catch a few hours sleep before work. Sometimes they were longer, a page's worth or more. These are the ones she likes to read as she waits. They remind her of him. They keep her focused on what she's doing.

Tonight she read a favorite. It starts a few pages after a description of her third birthday.

Friday. August 11th.

I hope you don't call the authorities on me after today. Even if you do, it was worth it. Christy and I made up a game at the park this morning. She stands on a picnic table and raises her hands out at her sides and falls backwards into my arms. She gets a little scared but she laughs every time I grab her.

It's called the "fall-backwards-thing".

After lunch, she was playing in the playground with these two snotty girls from Huntington Beach. They kept bragging about how they were NEIGHBORS and how they were FIVE. At one point, they were trying to stick it to Christy about how they could climb things ALL BY THEMSELVES despite the fact that Christy was just as agile as they were, maybe more. I said, "Christy, you want to do the fall-backwards-thing?" Snotty Girl #1: "What's the fall-backwards-thing?"

Christy surprised me by climbing all the way to the top of the biggest slide! Onto the part ABOVE the slide! 15 feet up or more! She put her hands out and she dropped like a falling angel. I caught her at my knees. "You girls want to do it?" I said.

"NOOOOOOOOOOOOOOOOOOOOOOOOOOOOO!" they *screamed! I love my niece.*

She closes the book and her eyes. She tries to remember, to live that time again. She wants so badly to be back there on the playground, to feel what that felt like, falling and knowing that Uncle Mickey would catch her.

Headlights.

A car. No! A van. The words "LOCKSMITH" and a phone number. It's 818. The van stops a dozen feet down the road and two guys get out.

The smaller of the two pulls on the van's sliding door. "Hey dumb-dumb, it's locked from inside!"

The bigger guy climbs back in. He shouts - his voice is oddly pitched and indistinct. She's heard people who can't hear well talk like this.

The door opens and black plastic bags tumble from the dark interior. The big guy follows. He's tall, thick. Sweat-wet hair bothers the scar from forehead to chin.

His partner is smaller—a shadow seems to follow his face—a voice barks from inside.

"You parked too far from the cliff!"

He drags a bag to the edge of the road. Grunting, he swings and heaves it down the steep incline. It makes a sloshing sound as it careens into the darkness.

The big guy hefts a bag. It tears and blood splashes his jeans. His curse is also a moan. The bag splits and severed body parts pour out. Dark puddles form in the dirt.

This makes shadow man laugh. He stoops and grabs something fleshy. He tosses it at the big guy. Moaning protestations. "Nooo! Nooo!" and "Skye!"

Skye tosses more bloody limbs. "Stop it," he shouts in a mocking soprano. *"I don't like it! I don't want to play with you anymore."*

Christy has often thought about this moment, when these hours of waiting would pay off, and she'd be face to face with the killers. She figured she'd be scared and she is. But she prayed that she would be confident. And she is. The years of training have prepared her. Every part of her mind and body is filled with a complete and utter confidence that she can beat these men and make them pay for killing her uncle.

Until they split up.

"Peter! There's something in the shadows there!"

The big one is gone. She scans the road, the hillside, the trees. She catches a glimpse of something moving. He's circling around behind her.

Skye is moving in a crouch, taking a short step then freezing, holding his breath, listening. He has something shiny in his hands. He steps and freezes. Steps and freezes.

She struggles to control her own breathing.

A gush of wind tugs at her hair. She looks down. A small boy stands next to her, naked and silent. Through his thick, wild hair she can see his dark eyes. He's peering up at her.

He steps from the shadows of the trees and into the open. His skin catches the moonlight and glows. He's the most beautiful thing she has ever seen. She takes a deep breath and joins him in the light.

"What the fuck!" Skye is no longer crouching. Peter appears at his side. They stare.

Christy can't know what they think of the little girl in her drill team uniform and the naked boy at her side. She can't know what they expect will happen next.

She leaps. Her elbow catches Peter in the neck. Her fist finds the center of the shadow of Skye's face. They scream and she screams just as loud.

Everything is motion. It feels like dancing. Her body performs a dance routine she memorized long ago. The dances steps are painted all around her. All she has to do is move her hands and feet to the waiting destinations.

Peter slips on the bloody ground and scrambles on hands and knees. More blood pours from his face. Skye slips and slides backwards. His frustration finds a voice that's pitched between a growl and a wail.

She isn't slipping. Her feet have left the ground. She's kicking now, her feet finding the killers in the dark, hurting them, punishing them, destroying them.

All the while, it's like she's falling, falling, her hands and feet reaching away from her, extending out forever, the little boy standing below, the light touch of his arms as he catches her.

She can feel every part of it. She's back at the playground now. She's in Uncle Mickey's arms. She's safe.

She opens her eyes just in time to see Skye pitch backwards, swallowed alive by a dark hole in the earth. Peter blindly rushes after him, and he too tumbles into the ancient hole. The burn scars are covered by vegetation but the hole is still deep and the fall is deadly.

Christy and the boy stand at the lip. It's now a grave. She takes his hand.

She is glad for many things at that moment. But most of all, she is glad that Uncle Mickey taught her Morse code. The boy's pulse pounds out a message.

S. A. F. E.

PRESCHOOL

XXXX

Every Monday morning, there are fewer kids. Today, it's Kenny and Lenny, the twins. Their mom, Janice, hadn't called or emailed and she wouldn't. Just like with Lilith last week, and Brendan and Dash the week before.

Teacher Adrianna scans the playground. There is still a good group, 8 Pescaditos and 6 Delphines. Two- and three-year-olds are in the Pescaditos. Four- and five-year-olds are Delphines. She sees Dana parking her car—that means Ezra and Milo will be joining the older group.

A stone-covered gully divides the playground from a road that snakes through the park. There is an old stone bridge, probably part of FDR's public works program, and Dana is hardly half way across when she starts talking.

"Big surprise. It's a Starbucks!" She digs through her purse with one hand while the other checks a text on her phone. Brendan and Milo head straight for the playground and start tossing sand. "It's all gone. The classrooms. The cubbies. The Caring Wall. Even the mural."

"Oh, I'd hoped they would leave that." Teacher Adrianna produces two identical yellow wiffle balls, one for each brother, defusing the escalating sand fight. "Teacher Lynn painted that the first year of the school, back in 1982."

"There's no room in the world for small, delicate things. It's all money, money, money. New, new, new!"

"There will always be a place for the children." She waves her hand over the little part of the park she has claimed for the school. Besides the sand lot and jungle gym, there is an old structure nearby with a working toilet. A dozen yards beyond that stands a small patch of trees. Teacher Adrianna has spread blankets under a low-slung canopy. They are far enough from the Ferndell entrance to the park that traffic sounds are light.

Sure, there's a hiking trail right through the center, and other children who aren't part of the school sometimes play on the jungle gym, creating confusion. But, it's a place to go. No permits. No problems, so far.

"Well, you're a hero, Teacher Adrianna. The Learning Lair is *needed,* it is *necessary.* It's a tradition. Brendan and Milo aren't going anywhere!"

Teacher Adrianna smiles. Janice said more or less the same thing last week. She'd been waitlisted for All Creatures Great and Small so maybe she moved the kids there.

"Besides, there's some magic here. Don't you feel it?" Dana shivers dramatically and heads back over the bridge.

The class is playing Counting Circus with colored scarves under the canopy when Lucas starts crying. Teacher Adrianna has been expecting it. Kenny and Lucas had been close. Arlo's dad called them the Three Musketeers and Arlo had disappeared the previous Friday.

She decides to skip Creeping and Crawling and go right to story time. Stories soothe this bunch, especially lonely Lucas. Besides, it is getting too hot for a hike up the gully. Maybe they will nap after the story and she can set up the afternoon activities. There used to be a schedule for parent volunteers to help with that, but this tradition has apparently been left at the old location.

Teacher Adrianna claps her hands. "Criss-cross applesauce!" The kids echo her words and dutifully arrange themselves in a circle, legs crossed beneath them. "Who wants to pick a book?"

Finny raises her hand. "Can I do something different?"

Teacher Adrianna brightens. Finny is one of the oldest kids, nearly five, and comes from a family of alumni—three older sisters attended the Learning Lair before her. So had her stepfather when he was little and the neighborhood was not as safe. "What do you have in mind, Finny?"

"I make up a story."

Finny has never done this before, but it isn't out of character. Always the first to jump into a new project, Finny has bright blue eyes that seems to absorb everything and everyone around her. She is naturally nurturing and has helped many of the kids here get through Drop-off Time during the tough first weeks of school. She is one of Teacher Adrianna's favorites.

"Go ahead, Finny."

The small girl arranges herself, hands spread out from her sides, fingers splayed over the blanket.

"There is a lady that drives a police car. Her daddy and her lived here for twenty days. In at tent. She was a baby in the park. She drives her police car every day and she waves at the park."

Finny waves at a passing car. Some hikers with a big white dog skirt the circle, looking guilty about interrupting.

"Okay, I tell another one?"

"Okay, Finny."

"There is a lady who draws at the telescope place. She draws a picture of a boy every day. He has big eyes. He lives in the park.

He is very dirty. He is very special. One day, she draws a different picture. She draws a picture of a man and she is going to marry him."

Teacher Adrianna is lost in the image. She too has seen the boy. Once, while cleaning up after everyone had left. She could still see his eyes.

"More?"

Teacher Adrianna nods, "yes."

For the rest of the day, Finny tells her stories.

She tells them a story about people making a movie. It's about boys who race cars and fight with knives. Somebody sees something that scares them and then someone else sees it. And pretty soon everyone is scared so they turn their lights all the way up and people can see them shining all over the city.

There's a story about a little girl named Miriam who rides a train in circles, waiting for her daddy to put out the fires and make it safe to come home.

About three brothers who got lost in the wild woods of the Ozarks. How the youngest brother disappeared and their dad would not let them have a funeral, since Jeffrey was never found. How every year, the two remaining brothers climb the hill behind the jungle gym and cry and shout Jeffrey's name until they are hoarse.

She tells them about a girl sitting in a box in Upstate New York, shivering away her college work hours, pretending to be a security guard while really watching the snowy trees for signs of a Cape May Warbler. Her boyfriend plays "I Love a Man in a Uniform" on the college radio station, and she imagines taking him to California for Christmas break. She imagines the warm house, her little sister who hates the nickname 'Munch', showing him Hollywood Boulevard, taking him to Bronson Cave, holding hands in the dark.

About a soldier in a parade through Paris about how the war is over. But inside his mind, he is really back in the gully and his bare feet are running across the smooth stones.

She tells them about Stevie and his drums and a car on fire.

She tells them about a girl named Bonnie who walks by the gully and sings a song. *"The creek is a bubbling and the birds a singing, and it sounds like music they know so well, just a boy and a girl, holding hands and dancing, beneath the trees at ol Ferndell."*

Teacher Adrianna listens, eyes fixed on the ground. When she finally looks up, it's nearly dark. The rest of the kids are gone. Finny says, "there's my mom. Bye."

And she too is gone.

ABOUT THE AUTHORS

TIM KIRK is a writer and filmmaker living two miles from Griffith Park. He is the author of the multi-generational Western novel, *Burnt*. His films include *Sex Madness Revealed, Director's Commentary: Terror of Frankenstein*, and *Bewitched*. He has produced *Room 237, The Nightmare, And With Him Came The West*, episodes of *Tom Explores Los Angeles*, and *The El Duce Tapes*.

DAVID CARPENTER (Rails) is a 4th generation Californian who has worked as a journalist, screenwriter, and university administrator, but who prefers playing in a band and in the ocean. He was a founding member of the Facebook group "People Named David Carpenter," now defunct.

PATRICK COOPER (Carousel) writes fiction which has appeared in numerous print and online outlets. He cowrote the 2018 film *Sex Madness Revealed*. He is the author of *Aren't You Gonna Die Someday? Elaine May's MIKEY AND NICKY: An Examination, Reflection and Making Of*. He lives in Eastern Pennsylvania with his wife and dog.

JOSH LAWSON (Billy Clover) resides in a sawmill town in Northern California where he collects and listens to the obscure and tragic music that lives in this story.

STEVE NEWMAN (Where's Farrell?) was born and raised in New York City, just outside Central Park.

TIM DAVIS (Last Hike at Bee Rock) is first, foremost, and forever a father. Writing in a wide range of medium (from radio, TV and film, to BSU video games, birthday songs and all manner of bloggery) helped him initially fill the time before his kids arrived, and has continued to provide a consistently arduous, occasionally gainful means of occupying his non-parental hours. His contribution to this anthology allowed him the opportunity to track his kids' journeys on this planet... and reflect on his own.

ROB ZABRECKY (Gold Star for Robbie) was once dubbed "one of LA's most interesting natives" by the LA Weekly. He is a musician (Possum Dixon), a magician who performs regularly at the Magic Castle and around the world, an actor appearing in *Ghost Story* and *Strange Angel* among other film and television, and the author of a memoir *Strange Cures*.

CPSIA information can be obtained
at www.ICGtesting.com
Printed in the USA
BVHW071440240619
551796BV00007B/1234/P